NAVARRO

NAVARRO

CARSE BOYD

CUTTING EDGE

ISBN-13: 978-1-952138-79-9

Published by
Cutting Edge Books
PO Box 8212
Calabasas, CA 91372
www.cuttingedgebooks.com

CHAPTER ONE

1

IT'S ABOUT these two men who came riding over the ridge and down into the valley east of Ajo, at dusk, a hundred and ten years ago. It's about what happened to them, and why, and what it meant, if it meant anything. You don't have faces like that, unless it meant something to you. It's a story about Sonny and Brother, at least he was called Brother, not caring much for the name Adrian, as who could blame him.

2

Having an outlaw in the family, even a small outlaw, isn't convenient at the time, but after a hundred years, you'd be surprised, it's a considerable distinction. That's what Sonny was: an outlaw. Or anyhow what he became. One of the New Mexico Gores plugged Sonny in '68, being sheriff at the time.

Sonny was a Henshaw. The Henshaws lived in southeastern Arizona, down along what's now the Mexican border. That big country down there, between Ajo and Douglas, just rambles along in its own sweet way, and to look at it, you'd never think anything happened there. It's grazing country. In the spring it's emerald and rich, and there isn't a town, there isn't a house for miles. It's lived-in country, though, and has been, ever since the forties. It just isn't lived in much. It hasn't changed. It was just like this in 1855.

Off the range, out in back, in the waterless land, that's where the Indians were, in places like Bapchule, Gu Achi, and Topawa. They were pretty quiet Indians. The Apaches were farther east and didn't come this way much. The Henshaws lived at Quijotoa, only they called it Covered Wells. Not counting a couple of Mexican villages, the nearest towns were Fort Tucson, 80 miles north, and Nogales, 140 miles south, which was a real town. The nearest neighbors, the Cunninghams, had a spread 10 miles over.

If there hadn't been the five of them, and if Sis hadn't been so close to the Cunningham girls, it would have been a lonely life. As it was, they got on fine.

Pa Henshaw was a ship chandler from Troy, New York, who'd come out West in '40, after his business failed. He was thirty-three then, but he must have had some kick to him, because Annie, his wife, was an exdance-hall girl he'd picked up in St. Jo. She was Scottish, and just as much of a character as he was, but less apt to talk her head off, and much more spry. She'd kept her looks, and she'd made a good wife out there.

What Pa Henshaw had aimed to do was open a general store, but once he got out to Quijotoa and found the land going begging, instead of settling down to sell seed and grain and smallclothes at Fort Tucson or some place like that, he built a shed over the water supply, renamed the place Covered Wells, and opened a trading post. You didn't need much ready cash back then, and he did all right. What he didn't do was set up any kind of ranch. He had one thousand acres of good range land, and all he did was sit on it. Annie couldn't understand that. She wasn't ambitious exactly, but she didn't see any point in throwing a good thing away either. But Pa wouldn't budge. He liked the silence. He liked the Indians. He liked the solitude. He blinked and seemed content. But though you'd never guess it, except when she drew her mouth down, Annie hated all three. If it hadn't been for the Cunninghams and her own kids, Annie would have gone mad out there. What Annie liked was company and a party once in a while.

They had three kids. Adrian, the oldest, was twenty-six and looked thirty at the time things began going wrong for the family. Annie didn't understand Adrian too well. She didn't like calling him Brother, either. Adrian was a perfectly good family name. She didn't see why he wouldn't use it. Sonny was a wild eighteen but seemed younger, Sis was sixteen, and Sis was Sis. She was going to be a pretty girl, though. Sonny was Annie's favorite. He had some get up and go to him, and he wasn't far away all the time, the way Adrian was. Adrian scared her sometimes. Whereas Sonny took after her. He was a great big, shambling boy who didn't know what to do with himself half the time, proud as hell, and twice as stubborn. He wasn't a big man, but he towered over her all the same. She was a very small woman.

There was a big difference between those who came out to settle the West, and those who were born and raised there. It wasn't something you could exactly put your finger on, but it was there, all right. They had a different, far horizon look in their eyes. So even though Brother seemed to take after Pa Henshaw, he had different ideas, and when he was fifteen he rode over to confabulate with the Cunninghams, came back with twenty head of cattle, and set the place up as a ranch, whether Pa wanted it that way or not. Pa never did get used to running a trading post smack in the middle of a ranch, but there wasn't much he could do about it. He just sat there and blinked, and let the damn thing grow up around him. There wasn't any doubt in anybody's mind whose ranch it was, either. It was Adrian's spread, all the way. He intended to run it as a business, and he didn't want any partners. Not that Brother was a hard man, but what was his was his.

Annie didn't understand Brother, but she was proud of him, and that left Sonny and Sis sort of out in the cold.

Sonny and Brother had their fights, practically every day. Sonny felt himself getting eased out and didn't fancy winding up as a hired hand. The thing that kept them from splitting apart was Sis. Sis was Ma all over again, but twenty-two years younger;

at sixteen she was already a lot prettier than the Cunningham girls, and besides, she just naturally had a way with her. She made the wheels go round. She was the apple of Pa Henshaw's eye, and she made life less lonesome for Annie. She knew how to cool Sonny down, in fact she was the only person who could cool Sonny down, and she was the only one of them who could handle Brother too. Though Ma and Sis and Sonny all blew their tops whenever they felt like it and forgot about it straight afterwards, Brother never said much; he took after Pa that way, so it was hard to tell what he was thinking most of the time. As for what he was feeling, nobody ever knew that. Brother kept himself to himself.

That spring day in March 1855, Brother was away at Fort Tucson, or so he'd said, and no telling when he would be back, for he aimed to do some hunting in the hills on the way home, that being his recreation. Ma and Sis were running up a dress for some kind of shebang the Cunninghams had planned for Saturday; and what Pa was doing nobody knew. He never left the store, anyhow. It was cool in the store. He liked it there.

So Sonny was the one who started the whole thing off, not that he meant any harm, but Sonny was one of those conspicuous people who just naturally manage to acquire trouble, the way other people have luck.

He just plain didn't know what to do with himself half the time except to take orders from Brother, maybe. Brother was all right, despite the fancy name, but when it came to the ranch, he wasn't a brother any more, he acted like a straw boss. It was do this, do that, and thanks for your advice, but I'm not having any; I don't think you've got the sense God gave mules anyway. Not that he wouldn't have cut off his arm to get you out of a mess, if you were in one. They were Henshaws. They might have a tug of war over the ranch, but when it came to the world outside, they hauled themselves together and pulled one way. Just the same, Sonny felt a lot better with Brother out of sight. Something inside him let out a yell, and he hightailed it into the back country, full of beans and looking for trouble.

3

Long about midafternoon he found it.

A thousand acres isn't the biggest spread in the world, but on the other hand, you couldn't exactly call it small, either. It wasn't fenced. Brother's small herd and the Cunningham cattle wandered where they wanted to. People were in short supply in that country in those days. Besides, ranching wasn't profitable yet, and the thirteen dollars a month you had to pay the hired help didn't come out of nowhere.

Which meant that pretty well, Sonny had the range to himself. He and Sis had spent their childhood wandering over this country. Going alone wasn't so much fun, but he knew where he was headed. He was headed where they always went. Right on the border of Henshaw land, on the Cunningham side, was a spring they'd privately christened Aztec Wells, for no reason in particular. They'd been going there ever since they were knee-high to a grasshopper and first learned to ride. Annie used to take them out there for picnics until they were old enough to go alone and had graduated from the buggy to the Appaloosas which Pa liked to keep round the place, though Appaloosas were Indian stuff, and not rightly a real horse at all.

At the moment, Sonny had Jackson, who was practically a quarter horse if the light was right and you didn't look too close. Jackson was okay.

That country east of Ajo, after the mountains fall back, it's a big, tilted, sky-riding plateau that rolls and ripples between the hills, like water down a draw after a cloudburst. The air's deceptive. It gives everything a halo. You practically never hear a bird. Farther east still, the cactus wren sits in the cactus, but the Henshaw land didn't have any cactus. It didn't have much by way of trees either, except bottle bush and a lone cottonwood or two at Aztec Wells. That's why Annie liked Aztec Wells. She had an affection for trees and had put some scrub pine round the house, but they didn't take, not even after she'd rigged up muslin canopies over them to keep the sun off.

Sonny couldn't feel any breeze, but there must be some somewhere, because the upland was full of those go-devils that whirl out of nowhere, full of sand and hotter than the air around them, and throwing the ghosts of sagebrush in your face. He amused himself for a while by chasing them and then riding through them. He always had liked to do that. It gave him a funny feeling.

Long about three, when he was real bored, he hit Aztec Wells. It was behind a butte that stuck up out of the ground for no particular reason. There was a broken-rock talus round the foot of the butte. It was hard going, but ten years of riding there had broken down some kind of a trail. You followed the trail round the left side of the butte to the back, where the ground was scooped out into a hollow. The spring itself was at the base of the butte, but dribbled down the talus, disappeared for a while, came out as a ripple of water over hot stones, and then widened into a tank. For about six feet on each side of the tank the ground was soggy with green grass that never did turn yellow, the cottonwood hung over the water, the bottle bush stood up between the blank sand and the green grass. It wasn't just a pretty spot. It was a blessing in all that heat.

He came round the bend, not expecting anything in particular, and then he saw the horses, three of them, and Mex, to judge by the saddles. Two men were down in the water hole, taking a bath. The third one he couldn't see.

Right away he wanted them out of there. He didn't like Mexes. No white man round there did. Not on his land anyhow.

Besides, he was bored, and he saw how to have some fun out of them. They hadn't heard him coming, and they were too busy splashing naked in the middle of that tank to be able to make for shore and their gun belts before he was on top of them. He never went anywhere without his rifle. In those days it wasn't a wise thing to do. He unlimbered it, nudged Jackson down to the shore, and just plain shot them out of the water. He didn't have any intention of hitting them, but they couldn't know that. At first they were so surprised, they just stared, while the bullets hit the water with a plop, as though a stone were skipping across the surface. Then they lit out. He didn't make it easy for them. He shot beyond them, so they had to change course. One of them stumbled and went under before he could get up again. What Sonny aimed to do was keep them away from their gun belts. It wasn't hard.

At the same time, his aim wasn't so good, because he just about died laughing. No Mexican ever likes to take all his clothes off at one time. That wouldn't be decent. So their water-soaked heavy woolen drawers weighed them down some. He'd never seen anybody look so scared.

Sonny just whooped it up. He didn't mean no harm.

"Navarro," they yelled.

There wasn't any answer, but Sonny whirled Jackson round, in time to see the bottle bush rustling.

"Navarro." The other two were on the other side of the pond. He didn't have to worry about them.

"Okay, come out of there."

Nothing happened. Then a bullet knicked into his saddle. Sonny didn't care for that. That saddle had cost a lot of money.

"I said come out." On the other side of the pond the Mexicans were knackering at each other in fast Spanish and trying to edge towards their guns. Sonny felt pretty mad, plunged Jackson into the thicket, and the third Mexican got up so fast, he was practically under the horse. He was a short, brawny Mexican, just beginning to go to fat, with a cruel, greasy face, heavy black mustaches, and a sugar-loaf sombrero on his head. He wasn't somebody you'd forget in a hurry. He looked mean, and he'd come up swearing. All Sonny got was a quick look while he reached out of the saddle and knocked the gun out of the guy's hand. He knew enough Spanish to know what the guy was saying, and he didn't take kindly to being cussed out by no Mex. He could see now why the Mex had been hampered, though. He'd been taking a crap, and his tight pants were half round his knees, so he couldn't move so good. It was too close quarters for a rifle. Sonny reared Jackson and chased him out into the open that way, holding onto his pants, waddling for all he was worth.

It was pretty comical, but right then Sonny didn't see it that way.

"Okay," he said, "git."

Navarro said exactly what would happen to anybody who treated Navarro that way. The other two wanted their guns back.

It made Sonny plain mad. "I said pull your pants up and git," he told them. He drew rein and reloaded and after one more shot, they got. Just to make sure they did, he jumped down and fired their own pistols after them. Come to think of it, now it was over, it had been pretty funny, he guessed. But by the time he was half home he had forgotten all about it.

CHAPTER TWO

Sonny got back to the ranch house long about six. There wasn't anything unusual about that. Supper was at five-thirty and Pa Henshaw liked his family as prompt as his meals.

So naturally Sonny made a point of being late. That was how Sonny was. He had to show he was grown-up some way.

Since that was the last day they ever were happy, it's maybe worthwhile seeing how they looked. Since they were all photographed in '54 that's not so hard. It's quite a picture. It must have been taken at Fort Tucson, by an army photographer picking up a little cash on the side.

Every one of them looks a heller, in his own style. Pa Henshaw's sitting in the middle. He looks like an intelligent manatee, in a dark shirt, a satin cravat, and his big hands in his lap. Annie is standing to his left. She looks more like his daughter than his wife. She has a flat white face, narrow eyes, and bangs over her forehead. It's a nice face, determined to get what it wants, and she's proud of that polka-dot blouse she's wearing. Sis is standing behind Annie. You can't see her very well. She's a carbon copy of Annie, but younger, taller, and more of a tomboy. She doesn't look as though she felt right in that black silk dress she has on. They all look pleased, except Adrian, but Sis is the only one who looks as though what she really wanted to do was giggle.

Adrian's the only one who looks like Pa, dark hair, a square jaw, and a determined expression. He's taller than Pa, but not as tall as Sonny. He looks as though he had better things on his mind than having his picture taken. But then Brother always did have a lot on his mind. Maybe that's why he never did talk much.

And then, on the left, there's Jonathan Paul, Jr., which is to say, Sonny himself. He's wearing Quapa Indian beaded gauntlets, God knows where he picked those up, gambler's pants, and the biggest round Stetson you ever saw. He's got an arrogant, distant look, he's a good foot taller than his parents, he wears his gun, pearl handle and all, slung low and almost over his groin, he takes after Annie all right, and you can practically hear his flat drawl. It's obvious he doesn't know what to do with himself, and the others don't know what to do with him either, but he's going to do something, you can bet your life on that.

So there they are, just any family on any ranch.

The ranch house was built Texas style but was bigger than most, Pa Henshaw having a way with him when it came to getting Indians to work. On the other hand, since you never knew about Indians, the mud walls were thick, and the windows small and covered with heavy wooden shutters. That made the light a little on the dim side. The building on the right was the kitchen, but it had a bunkhouse behind it, where Sonny and Brother slept. The building on the left had a big parlor in it, a bedroom for Annie and Pa, and a shanty room tucked on, which was for Sis. Beyond that was a stable of sorts, with Annie's chicken yard attached. The floors were still dirt floors, except in the parlor, which was tile, and between the two main buildings was a space roofed over, where they kept everything that wouldn't fit any other place, which meant just about everything you could think of.

Sonny stabled his horse and ambled over to the kitchen house. It was almost dark, a nice night, but there was a green line along the horizon, and a wind in the air. It wasn't going to be a good night maybe after all. At night round here it got plenty cold, and the wind could slash your lungs out, even this late in the year. He rubbed his hands together, opened the kitchen door, and went clanking in.

Annie looked up with a frown. She didn't happen to share his partiality to heavy Mexican spurs, and she'd told him that before, not that it did any good. "We already started," she said, and put her mouth into a tight little Scots line. It was warm inside the kitchen, and dim. It took a while for his eyes to adjust. There weren't any chairs, just benches. He slung himself into his usual place.

Annie wasn't a bad cook, but it always made her worried to cook at all. At least he guessed that's why she was looking so worried. What she was best at was heavy strained soups, and meat was never in short supply. What they did lack was greens, or any fruit more ambitious than a shriveled up little winter apple, down from the loft of the stable. But it was amazing what Annie could do with a cooked apple. They were up to the apple now.

They weren't any of them long on talking, except Sis. It was Sis he missed right away. It didn't occur to him to say what he'd been up to himself. Annie never cared for that kind of hijinks until afterwards, and Pa and Brother didn't care for it at all. But he'd wanted to tell Sis about it. Sis had a sense of humor.

"She went over to the Cunninghams'," said Annie.

"She goes over to the Cunninghams' too damn much," said Sonny.

"Sonny. You know I don't like for you to swear."

"That wasn't swearing," said Sonny. "She does. She's always over there."

"Your sister's growing up, whether you know it or not. I'm glad she has the Cunningham girls for company. It's lonely for a girl out here."

"Who's she going to marry? The hired help?"

Annie flushed.

"You leave your mother alone," said Pa. "She's right. Sis can't spend the rest of her life riding hell for leather in all directions with her own brother. It ain't natural."

"What's that supposed to mean?"

"It isn't supposed to mean anything," said Annie. She sounded tired. "But I wish Adrian was here."

"What for?"

"I don't know," said Annie. "I just wish he was." She stuck more hay into the stove, that's what they had, a hay burner. There wasn't anything else they could burn. She had the second cylinder filled and ready, and shoved it in.

"She said she'd be back for dinner, that's all."

Sonny decided not to say anything about those Mexes. Besides, Sis stayed overnight at the Cunninghams' all the time. She practically lived there, as far as he could see.

"Seems to me Brother spends half his time out hunting these days," said Sonny. "I thought he was coming back today."

Pa sniggered, and Annie shushed him up.

Sonny glowered at them. He didn't like not to be told things.

"It isn't as if he ever caught anything worth mentioning."

"Maybe he's after bigger game," said Pa Henshaw.

"You poking fun at me?" Sonny looked puzzled.

"Oh shush up, both of you," said Annie. But she seemed to be listening to the silence and not liking it much.

Sonny got up and went outside. It was a clear night, but he couldn't hear anything. Somewhere at the back of his head those Mexicans bothered him. He didn't see why. They were probably thirty miles away by now. But they didn't have any right being in this neck of the woods at all. Usually they didn't come up this far.

When he went back into the kitchen, on the way to the bunkhouse, Pa had gone, but Annie was still sitting there, not doing anything in particular.

"There's nothing to worry about," he said, and stood there awkwardly. He'd have liked to put his arms around her, but he was at the wrong age for that.

"I'm not worried. I'm just resting," she said. "I'll be glad when your brother's back, that's all."

That was enough to stop any feelings Sonny may have had in the matter. He took off his boots and went to bed.

CHAPTER THREE

NAVARRO sat on a rock and picked his teeth. He was still plenty mad. He was also cold, hungry, and bored, and wished he'd never left Chihuahua, which was home base, two hundred and fifty miles away.

Navarro wasn't a man but an animal, and never could think more than ten minutes ahead. Those big northern Mexican provinces that even the Spanish had never been able to do anything with, arid, and dry, and treeless, where even the Indians were nothing but scavengers, bred fifty Navarros a day, and if they hadn't started killing each other off as soon as they could hold a knife, out of natural cussedness, they'd have made that whole country unlivable. As it was, the survivors rounded up a gang and lived on what they could steal, pretty high according to their own notions, killed each other off for the hell of it, and rode high until one of their own men got up enough courage to shoot them in the back and take over. There wasn't one of them who wasn't afraid of his own men. There wasn't one of them who wasn't trigger-happy so long as he could squat in ambush and feel safe.

That's what had Navarro jumpy. His men were getting out of hand. This trip north had been a mistake. The pickings had been slim, and Norte Americanos had a tendency to fight back that had killed one man already, and made raiding for a living tougher than it ever was back home.

The men were sitting behind him, drinking and laughing at him for what the gringo had done to him that day. He couldn't stand that. He knew he had to get them moving. But he couldn't get them moving yet. He didn't want to raid the ranch until everyone in it had gone to bed. That way he would take them by surprise.

Below them was a valley. You entered it by this trail across the rocks, with a sheer drop on one side, and piled up bits of butte on the other. Half a mile across the valley lay the ranch. The Cunningham ranch. There was a big barn, a stable, the house itself, a couple of corrals, sending long shadows in the early moonlight, and a smaller paddock where the horses were. It looked like a prosperous spread. If there wasn't anything else to take, they could drive off the horses and sell them across the border.

While he stood there, watching, a door opened, the light came seeping out, and a girl stepped through the door, stood talking a moment, and then walked off into the shadows to get her horse. The door closed. One but not all the lights went out at the windows. Pretty soon she was on her way. The night was so clear, the ground so cold, that hoofbeats of the horse tumbled over one another through the air. She was headed straight towards them at a brisk canter.

"What's that?" asked Pedro. Pedro was his second in command. Pedro was the one who always fed him questions.

"Just a girl."

"What she want?"

"Get down. Just get down that's all. We'll give her a surprise," said Navarro. He didn't mean anything by that at the time, his thoughts were still on the ranch, except maybe she might have something valuable, something worth having.

The horse sounded slower now. She must be at the bottom of the trail. They got down. He looked to see if they were well enough hidden, and then ducked down himself.

The trip up the trail was shorter than he thought. Before he had much time to think, the horse whinnied and snorted, blowing steam out of its nostrils, and was practically on top of him.

He jumped up and seized the bridle. The girl slashed at him with her crop. It stung across his face. He whistled, the others rose up around her, he reached up and dragged her to the ground and the horse broke away and cantered beyond them.

She didn't scream or anything. She did try to get away, but she didn't have a chance. He could see her now. She looked like the kid who'd made a fool out of him that morning. She must be his sister.

So he had a way of getting even for being made a fool of after all.

"Okay," he said, "let's have some fun with her." And being the leader, naturally went first.

Then she did scream. He couldn't have that. There was still the raid on the ranch to think of. He gagged her. She fought hard, but that only excited him. In the scuffle she ripped one of the buttons off of his shirt. He didn't even notice.

CHAPTER FOUR

ANNIE ALWAYS got up early, just before dawn, as a general rule, but this time something else had wakened her. She didn't know what. She lay there in the darkness listening to Pa snore. It wasn't quite darkness, of course. She got up, got herself into her everyday dress, and went through to the kitchen bunkhouse. It was what she did every morning; she was sleepy, she didn't notice anything, but at the back of her mind she didn't feel easy. She didn't know why. Her first job in the morning was getting the stove started. If the coals had gone out that wasn't easy. She raked them and saw they hadn't. So all she had to do was blow on them, add a few twigs, and shove a hay cylinder into place, and at least that was the first problem of the day solved. Somewhere outside their only rooster crowed. That was the second job, feed the chickens and draw water for breakfast. Feeding the chickens was something she always enjoyed. Not that she had much use for chickens one way or the other, but she never did have much time to herself, and she liked to stand out there, with the wind whipping her skirt, the first one up on a clear morning, and think about nothing in particular while she threw the grain out.

She got the grain, let herself outside, headed for the chicken pen, and that's when she saw the fire in the east. So the chickens didn't get fed that morning.

It never even crossed her head to fetch Pa. Pa was useless when it came to emergencies. He couldn't move fast enough. She went right through the kitchen, into the bunkhouse, and woke Sonny up. She didn't take half measures either. Half measures never got you anywhere with Sonny. She did what she'd always done to get him up, ever since he was a baby, hold his nose until he opened his mouth, and go right on holding it. It got him up all right.

"Now what did you want to go doing that for?" he asked.

"The Cunningham place is on fire. The whole sky's lit up."

He was still sleepy! "Let it burn," he said, and turned over.

"Sonny, you get right up and get over there. Your sister's over there. And Adrian isn't back, either."

That got him up all right. His white-stockinged feet were enormous. He got into his boots, slammed a hat on his head, and in five minutes he was on his way. He didn't even stop for coffee.

He was there in an hour. The Cunningham place was burning all right. In fact, except for one wing of the ranch, it was burnt out. What Annie had seen was a brush fire. The field was dry, sparks had lit it, and the whole land in front of him looked like a black and burnt mattress. The only flame now sat in the tufts on the Cunninghams' one charred scrub oak. Sonny hadn't passed anybody or anything on the way, hadn't expected to, and though he noticed the ground was scuffed up just before the trail turned down, he didn't make anything of it much. He was in too much of a hurry.

It didn't take him more than twenty minutes to make it to the Cunninghams. As soon as he could make out details, he could see why they were just standing around. All their horses had been run off. There wasn't any way to get anywhere. Not short of an afternoon's hike. There hadn't been anything they could do but wait for the Henshaws to come over.

The first person he saw in front of him was Adrian with smoke all over his face.

"What the hell happened?" asked Sonny. He was looking for Sis, but didn't see her. She might be inside what was left of the house. But somehow he had a sinking feeling that she wasn't.

"That tin horn Navarro," said Cunningham, a tight, short man, coming up to them. "He and his gang crossed the border three weeks ago. They've been raiding all through here," he spat. "If I could get my hands on him, he wouldn't live long. But he took care of that."

"It's a good thing Sis got out of here," said Adrian. "We got one of them anyhow."

"What do you mean Sis got out of here? Where is she?"

Adrian looked worried. "She left about eight, about an hour before I got here. Which was about when the trouble started."

Sonny could see the man they'd shot now. He was lying on his back, round the corner of the ruins of the barn. It was one of the men at the pool all right. He just looked down and didn't say anything. He couldn't. His stomach just about dropped out.

"She never got home," he said, and whirled the horse round. Adrian grabbed the reins.

"Hold it, Sonny," he said. "If anything's happened to Sis, I go too."

Sonny didn't pay any attention. Adrian jumped up behind him and landed hard. Brother was a solid man. The horse's rump and back legs went down with the shock, recovered, and then Sonny got out of there. He didn't bother to say anything. He was too scared.

The signs of what had gone on up at the pass were easy enough to see, once you knew what to look for, even if he had scuffed them up some coming through.

They could see where she'd been stopped, where they'd gotten her off her horse, where the horse had run away. There were boot marks everywhere, Mexican ones, to judge by the spur marks, and off to one side of the trail, the sage was broken and beaten down. That's where they must have attacked her.

"Don't tell Annie, that's all," said Sonny. "Just don't tell Annie."

Brother swore. "Maybe they took her with them," he said. It was about the last hope.

It was then they heard the damn-fool horse whinny, from down below them to the right somewhere, from the other side of the precipice. They had to scramble round a couple of boulders before they could see anything much.

"Is she down there?" Brother was shortsighted.

"Yes, she's down there," said Sonny.

"Dead?"

"She's lying on her face." He began to scramble down.

It took them over an hour to get back to the house. Annie was waiting for them. They could see her from a long way off, just standing alone in the yard, with her hands folded in front of her. When she saw the body slung over the horse, she turned and went into the kitchen. They were too far away to see the expression on her face. Then Pa came out, shielding his eyes with his hand.

There wasn't any point in telling Pa, either. He looked at them hopelessly. The way Sis's hands hung limp against the girth, you could tell at a glance she was dead.

"How?" asked Pa.

"Her horse threw her. On the pass."

Sonny tried to make it convincing, but his voice shook. "Don't let Ma see her until we get her cleaned up. She took quite a fall."

He and Brother got the body down and carried it into the respectable end of the house and laid her out. Her face hadn't been damaged, even though she had fallen on it, but the rest of her wasn't pretty.

"I guess when they got through they just threw her over that cliff," said Sonny.

"Or maybe she jumped." Brother hesitated. "I'll go get some water," he said. He headed for the door.

When he opened it, Annie was standing there, with a big cast-iron bucket of water. Brother couldn't look at her. All he saw was the steam from the water.

"I'll take it," he said. "Please, Ma."

She didn't even seem to see him there. She marched into the room.

"Get out, both of you," she said.

"Ma, you shouldn't ..."

"I said get out," she said. "You, too, Sonny. I mean it." It was the first time she had ever called him Sonny.

She didn't say anything else. She just waited until they left. Then she shut the door on them, and stayed in there maybe two and a half hours.

When at last she came out, her face was a white mask.

"She's been raped," she said.

They didn't know what to say to her.

"I said she's been raped. Do you think I don't know what men do? I should. I spent long enough learning."

Pa tried to come over to her.

"No," she said. "Leave me alone for a while. And you boys better go over to the Cunninghams. They'll need help."

"You shouldn't be alone, Ma."

Annie didn't cry. But she did begin to shake. "I *want* to be alone," she said. "Don't you understand that? We haven't even got the wood to bury her in. Not even a box. There's nothing in this country. Nothing in this country anywhere at all."

They buried Sis the next morning. Annie had wanted to do that at Aztec Wells, which wasn't any idea Sonny could face, but since they'd taken the old spring wagon apart to make a coffin, a job that kept Pa up all night so at least he could keep busy, they didn't have any way of getting the body that far. The Cunninghams came over. That was some help. But there wasn't a tree, there wasn't a preacher, there wasn't even a rise of ground, or a stone, or a fence.

Well, every family in that country had to start its graveyard sometime, but this one was too close to the house, not more than a thousand yards away, where you could see it out the window any time.

One thing, the earth out there is too yellow and too dry to look raw. It was one of those hot, clear, blue days that make you prickly all over. Annie had gone off by herself that morning. What she'd come back with was a cutting and some black dirt from Aztec Wells. It didn't do any good to tell her the plant would die.

"Something's going to grow in this godforsaken country, if I have to watch it day and night," she said. So Sonny scooped out a hole for the black earth, and the plant stood there now, under a canvas sunshade, held up by four sticks. It was wilting already in that open heat, and Annie never took her eyes off it once, not while Pa read out of an old thumbed copy of the English Book of Common Prayer, not even while the boys shoveled the adobe clods in, and stamped them down.

She'd go on watering it every morning, Sonny supposed, by herself, with a can of water from the pump, the way she always insisted on being alone while she fed the chickens, day after day, and getting older.

And it was all his fault. He looked at Brother, kept his mouth shut, and went back with the others to the house.

"We could get up a posse," said Cunningham. He had to say something.

"What good would that do?" asked Annie. She didn't sound as though she was exactly in the room with them.

"They've had two days' head start," said Brother. "Besides, you've got troubles of your own. Ma's right. It's done now. It can't be undone."

"Oh hell," said Sonny, and got out of there. And spent all day riding, riding towards Aztec Wells without realizing it, and then realizing it and coming back, until he couldn't stand it any more; he just went there and spent the whole day sitting, until after it was almost dark.

He could see those damn Mexes still there, in the pool, and what a lot of fun he'd thought he'd had with them. And the other one, the leader, with his pants half down and that lousy face of his. Navarro. And he could see Navarro getting to Sis first.

He took out of his pocket the thing he'd picked up at the pass, the thing he hadn't shown Brother, a small silver concha, with a turquoise stud in the middle of it. That guy in the shrubs had been wearing them. Those Mexes believe in dressing up real pretty. Standing up, he threw it into the pool and knew exactly what he was going to do. And he wasn't going to be stopped doing it either.

But better to wait till dawn.

The trouble was, when he got back to the house, he couldn't stand it. What do you say when you're to blame for a thing like that? What do you say when something like that happens, for that matter? He didn't know.

"You might at least try to talk to Annie," Brother told him. He didn't think much of Brother right then. Brother didn't even want to try to get them.

"I'm doing my best," said Sonny. And then just couldn't stand it any more. He got up, went into the bunkhouse and sat down to clean his rifle. Brother followed him on in and just watched that procedure. It got on Sonny's nerves. But he tried not to say anything. He just buckled on his gun, stuck his bowie knife in his boot, picked up the rifle, and got out of there.

"Where the hell do you think you're going?"

Sonny was in the kitchen by now. "I'm going after them. You won't do anything. And I'm going to get every last one of them, if hell freezes over," said Sonny, who didn't stop, but went right on walking out the door.

Annie didn't want him to go. What was the use? Losing Sis had been bad enough. What was the point of it?

Brother thought that over for a minute, and then went to get his own gear. Seeing the look on Annie's face, he hesitated, but not much.

He smiled that tight smile of his and just shrugged. "I'm going after him. Somebody's got to stop him falling on that thick head of his."

"But you can't. I've got to have someone. And you were getting married and all. I've never even seen her. I don't want to lose any more of you."

"You'll see her."

"I don't want to be here alone."

Pa winced. Brother tried not to notice.

"I said somebody's got to stop him falling on his thick head. Besides, in a way he's right. If Navarro gets away with it, we won't be safe to turn over in our beds."

"But that's none of your concern."

Adrian just left.

It took him three quarters of an hour to catch up with Sonny. The damn fool was trigger-happy and had his rifle out. Well, maybe you couldn't blame him at that. This country had become mighty unpeaceful all of a sudden.

"It's Brother," Adrian called, and rode up alongside.

"I'm not going back."

"Nobody asked you to."

"I don't want any help."

"It ain't what you want, it's what you got."

"You wouldn't even let me do this alone." Sonny sounded anguished.

"No, Son, I wouldn't. What's eatin' you anyway?"

"Nothin'." But there was. He didn't want Adrian to know what had caused it all. He didn't want anyone to know. He just wanted to blast it out of the ground, until he wasn't to blame any more.

The trouble with Brother was, he saw too much. And never said anything when he did, which was even worse.

And yet, in a way, he was glad of the company.

CHAPTER FIVE

I T WAS GETTING on towards dawn. The bandits had been traveling all night, through back trails no American would know about, and though the captured horses slowed them down some, Navarro didn't think he had much to worry about. He posted sentries and went to sleep.

Of course it was a pity about the man who'd been shot, Lopez. Navarro had been careful to look sorry about that. It was one of the secrets of his success. He always grieved. He'd grieved as a child and he'd gone right on grieving. He was nothing but a big, weeping baby, with a nasty, mean, narrow little mouth, and if he couldn't get what he wanted any other way, he drowned it in tears. It kept the men happy. And none of them was exactly going to miss Lopez anyway, not with all those horses, and one less way to split the take.

Dawn woke him up. By then he'd forgotten all about Lopez. So had the men. It was a matter now of getting the horses over the border, at Naco probably. There wasn't any closer place to take them. Naco was 180 miles away, Nogales was closer, but Navarro had his own reasons for not going to Nogales. Nogales was one of those places where even the Mexicans wanted his head in a noose. It was also too close to the American Dragoons at Tucson for comfort. There weren't any other towns in that country, and not a real town until you hit Chihuahua, which was well into Mexico. There was nothing but a dry, mountainous desert, bare hills, and poisonous heat. The border country itself was different. There were valleys hidden away there, with springs, and green grass, and a tree once in a while. That meant forage for the horses, so they couldn't keep too far away in the hills, if they wanted to keep the horses in shape. To get to Naco would take about seven or eight days.

On the sixth day they entered those steep hills which keep the San Migael Valley hidden from the world. There was even a river, one of the few rivers in that country that don't dry up every year so that if you want water you have to dig for it.

Navarro moved his men quietly. Some Americans had been sitting in that valley for ten years now, one big ranch, the Prentice place, with too many people round to make it safe to attack it with just fourteen men. But at the southern end of the main valley there was a little place called Lochiel, and that was where Navarro was heading. Long about dusk he reached it.

It wasn't much to look at. Just two or three empty adobes, mostly with the roof caved in and holes in the walls. Mexicans are always putting up adobes too big for them and then politely ignoring them while they fall down.

But one of the places was patched up, and a couple called Gusman lived there, an old man and his part-Indian wife, who was a lot younger. They'd have food stashed away somewhere. Gusman was known to be tightfisted and also ran a cantina of sorts. The men needed supplies, and besides, if you have fourteen men up against one old man, you don't have to ask for hospitality, you just take it. It would never have occurred to Navarro to do anything else.

He grinned and told the men to do exactly what they liked. He didn't think somehow the old man would put up much fight.

Nor did he.

CHAPTER SIX

NAVARRO HADN'T exactly been hard to track. Not with the horses and all those men. Sonny was a good tracker, whatever else he was, Brother was no slouch, and thanks to Pa Henshaw, who didn't believe in taking a highhanded attitude to Mexes just because you'd taken their land, both the boys knew enough Spanish to get around, and with Mexes that was a help too.

It was pretty clear that once he was clear of the Cunningham land, Navarro had gotten careless and wasn't worried about being followed. As far as Sonny was concerned, that was an advantage. He wasn't in any hurry. A good steady pace would bring them up to Navarro fast enough and would save the horses. Navarro had too much gear to outdistance two men without any. But then Brother began to get twitchy, the way he did sometimes.

Sonny put up with it for a while. "What's eating you?" he asked.

"Nothing in particular." Brother gave him a funny sideways look and then stared straight ahead.

"It wouldn't be we were gettin' too close for comfort, maybe?"

"No, it wouldn't be that." Brother didn't seem to be paying much attention. He was watching the ground for tracks. When he saw they went right and not left he gave a grunt, let out his breath, and straightened up. But he still looked worried.

"You can turn back if you want to." Sonny enjoyed needling Brother sometimes. Now he was practically on his own and had something to do, Sonny felt pretty good.

They'd come out of the canyon and could see a collection of adobes down below them.

"That's Lochiel," said Brother.

"You been here before?"

"Could be," said Brother, looking the place over. "Then again, on the other hand, maybe not."

Somebody had been through there all right. There were what looked remarkably like fresh bullet holes on the wall of one of the buildings, and fifteen men can't go through anywhere without leaving some traces. There was a wisp of smoke coming out of one building, but the door was shut and the windows shuttered. There was a pathetic little garden out in front, sunflowers mostly, and red geraniums. Mexicans are crazy about red geraniums, but these had taken a beating recently. They were all crushed down.

They both dismounted, Brother shouted, and got no answer. They could hear the creek rattling over its stones, fifty feet away.

"Well, it's lived in if anybody's alive," said Brother grimly, and rattled the door. It didn't give. It was bolted from the other side, by a cross beam probably.

"You damn fool, we're from the Prentice place," shouted Brother.

Sonny gave him a quick look. Brother seemed to know an awful lot about this neck of the woods, all of a sudden. Brother just stared back at him. After a while there was a movement inside, they heard the bar being taken down, and a scrawny old man stood there. He had a gash on his forehead, he was blinking, and he didn't look so good. Mexican, but mostly Spanish, by the looks of him. Come down in the world, probably, either that or never got back up.

Brother pushed by him, into the room. It was pretty dark in there. Once he was inside the door, Sonny couldn't even see him. All he could hear was the clank of his spurs. He got his gun out, and slid round the door, just waiting, until his eyes got used to the darkness.

"Some men went through here last night," said Brother.

"Yes, Señor." It was more a question than a statement. The man was scared.

The room was a shambles. It didn't take much imagination to see what had gone on there.

"So where did they go?"

"I do not know."

"I said where did they go?"

The man merely shrugged.

"Scared," said Brother to no one in particular.

"I reckon we could do a little scaring of our own," said Sonny, cocked his gun, and shot at the old man's feet.

"You goddam fool," said Brother, and slammed him against the wall.

"You shouldn't have done that."

Brother didn't even listen.

"I said you shouldn't have done that."

"What're you going to do about it," snapped Brother, and turned his back on him. He looked disgusted. "You'll get your licks in when the time comes. These are just old people, you damn fool."

That was when the woman came out of a shadowy door to the cook shack, they hadn't noticed before. Whatever else you had to say for her, she wasn't old. But she'd certainly had a going over.

The old man wouldn't even look at her. Sonny could sum that up all right.

"Your wife?"

"Sí, Señor." He sounded as though he were talking about the distant past. Mexicans were like that, usually. Whether it was the woman's fault or not, they never felt the same afterwards. One way you looked at it, that was a silly attitude. Another way, maybe it wasn't.

"Are you going to kill them?" asked the girl. She had a deep voice.

Brother gave her a hard stare and then nodded.

She rubbed her arms and thought that over. "They went to Naco," she said. "I heard them talking. Afterwards. You just follow the trail. The big fat one, Navarro. He's the dangerous one."

"Yeah," said Brother. "I gathered that. When'd they leave?"

"After dawn."

About fourteen hours' head start. But getting rid of the horses would slow them up some. "They have the horses?" he asked.

"Yes, they had the horses," she said. She sounded stunned.

One funny thing about Brother, he always seemed to think money did a lot more than it did. Maybe because he made his own money go a lot farther than it could ever have gotten by itself unaided. He put a couple of silver dollars down on a table and got out of there awkwardly.

At the end of the village they could pick the trail up okay. It wasn't traveled much, but it was traveled. It was perceptible. Brother didn't take it.

"You stay here," he said. "See if you can help them out."

"Where do you think you're going?"

"I've got business."

"Any reason why it isn't my business?"

"It isn't your business."

"I'm coming anyway."

Brother frowned. Quite clearly he didn't like the sound of that. But there wasn't much he could do about it, except get a little quieter than usual.

"What about Navarro?"

"He'll keep," said Brother, and didn't say anything else for the next hour.

CHAPTER SEVEN

S ONNY COULDN'T figure it out. Brother seemed to need him like a dog needs a can tied to its tail. They rode on for about an hour, always headed north.

"Seems like you know this country mighty well," said Sonny.

"I know where I'm going."

Brother always knew where he was going and never explained where it was. That was the way he was. It had never made him any easier to get on with. But Sonny didn't say anything about that. He just jogged on behind, feeling madder than a hornet.

The hills leveled off on either side of them rapidly, like a wave after the crest has broken in the middle, and there ahead of them was a big upland valley, bright green with watered grass and the mountains which hemmed it in ten or fifteen miles away. There were even one or two trees. On a knoll about four miles away was a low, verandaed, big house, built shotgun style, with a high, pitched roof.

Brother looked round for tracks, seemed relieved, didn't seem to know whether to ride on or turn back, gave Sonny a queer look, shrugged his shoulders, and went on after all. Sonny wasn't taken in by that little performance. When Brother had something he didn't want you to know, he didn't just get bashful. He got downright sly. And asking him a direct question usually didn't help much either. All you got out of asking a direct question was a long, long silence, and a plaintive, pitying look directed out of those transparent eyes, up at the horizon. Brother bore with other people's curiosity quite well, considering. But you couldn't exactly say he went out of his way to satisfy it.

"You wouldn't want to tell me where we are, of course," said Sonny, just to needle him.

After some considerable thought, Brother seemed to feel it was okay to let out that much information anyhow. "It's the Prentice place," he said.

"Friends of yours?"

"I thought they might know something," said Brother.

There didn't seem to be anybody around much, unless you counted a few cattle. Fat, sleek cattle at that. The land was so rich it practically made you sick just to look at it.

After a while they got within hailing distance of the house. There was a woman of about fifty on the porch.

She turned to the doorway. "It's Adrian," she called.

"Well, at least you're acquainted," said Sonny.

"It's nice to have you back, but we didn't expect you," said the woman. She looked at Sonny curiously.

"My brother," said Adrian. "My kid brother."

"Really, Adrian, you are the limit. I thought when you said kid brother, you meant someone about four feet tall."

Adrian smiled. The idea seemed to amuse him. "This is Sonny. He's bigger."

"Quite a lot bigger," said Mrs. Prentice dryly. "Well, come on up. And I'll tell Molly. I expect you're hungry."

Brother looked sheepish. But he allowed as how, yes, maybe he might be a little hungry. Mrs. Prentice seemed to know Brother pretty well. She laughed at him and then went into the house, just as Mr. Prentice came out. Mr. Prentice was a big man, made a little soft by age, but still, there was no denying who it was that ran things round there.

"Well, Molly'll be glad to see you, but I guess that isn't what brought you round," said Prentice.

Brother told them what had brought them round.

Prentice didn't offer sympathy. He just chewed his lip for a moment and then asked if they needed help.

Brother said it was something he had to do alone.

That made Sonny mad.

"I thought maybe they might have been bothering you," said Brother.

"No," said Prentice. "We didn't even know they were round here. It's a good thing. The boys are up at the north end. Except Jake, and Jake isn't good for much but cutting wood and helping out in the kitchen. You may as well stay to supper. Stay the night if you like. But I guess maybe you'll want to go on. Why don't you go see Molly?"

"I'd like to wash up first."

Prentice grinned. "Well you know where things are. I'll tell Jake to bring some hot water."

He left them, and Brother ambled through the hall, into what was obviously a guest room, and pretty too. It was a real house.

"What're the sons like?" asked Sonny.

"What sons?"

"The boys."

"He just meant the hired help. He doesn't have any sons."

Sonny thought that over for a while.

"And Molly?"

Brother was washing his face. Jake had come and gone by then. Jake turned out to be colored, but he wasn't a houseboy or anything, just a broken-down hired hand, who looked as though he'd fallen off too many horses. There were a few colored cow-hands, even in those days.

"Daughter," said Brother.

"You seem tol'rable well acquainted."

"Prentice and I get on," said Brother. "Stop asking damn-fool questions."

Sonny sloped off into the hall. Brother was beginning to get him down, as usual. He acted so grown-up and know-it-all, and he wasn't that much older. The hall was wide and ran right through the house. On a hot day it kept the place cool. Now, towards evening, it was shadowy, and nobody had lit any lamps yet. It was the fanciest house he'd ever been in, and it made him awkward. It was the sort of place he would have liked himself, now he'd seen it. And knew he would never have, now he'd seen it. Sonny knew there were a lot of things he couldn't have, and knowing that always made him restless. There was a big, half-length mirror in a gilt mahogany frame. He looked himself over. You didn't often see a mirror that big outside of a fancy house, either, and he'd only been to a fancy house once in his life, and if you came right down to it, it hadn't even been particularly fancy.

Exciting enough, though, if you were just drunk enough and got out before you got disgusted. Sonny liked what he saw in the mirror a good deal more than he liked himself. That guy in the mirror, now, looked fine and could probably get anything he wanted. Which was fine for him, but in some ways Sonny had the suspicion he couldn't though he didn't exactly know why not.

One thing that was for sure, he was a lot better looking than Brother. Sonny wouldn't have wanted to look like Brother much. And for some reason he wondered what Annie was doing and thinking about, back alone at the ranch with Pa. Annie must have been a pretty woman when she was younger. He'd never thought about that before, but thinking about it now made him mad. He shrugged, looked around him, and followed the cooking smells which had been inviting him for some time, through a real dining room, and into the kitchen. The kitchen was big and shadowy, but an oil lamp on the table was lit. There was nobody there, except a young girl in a sprigged dress, leaning over the wood stove, filching a tray of biscuits out of the oven, with those quick, exasperated movements women use when the tray is too hot and the rag is too thin, but they never think to double up the rag, so maybe they enjoy it. She straightened up, turned, and saw him.

"You gave me a start. You must be Sonny. Adrian's brother," she said, and smiled. She was a slim, tall girl, very assured, with clear, distant eyes, and an amused but sympathetic expression. "I'm Molly," she said, looked as though she was going to hold out her hand, clearly decided that would embarrass him, and went back to fussing with the biscuits instead.

"That's right, ma'am," said Sonny, which settled their relations right there. It wasn't just that he was in awe of her. It was that she had Sis's voice. He hadn't thought of Sis in three or four days, he realized, he'd been too busy getting after Navarro. Now that voice brought her back. He'd always taken Sis for granted and relaxed with her and nobody else, but now he realized he had loved her as well.

And this girl, at first sight. They even moved the same way.

Molly smiled encouragingly, and then, quite suddenly, blushed.

"Oh dear," she said. She sounded mildly concerned.

Sonny was abashed.

"I burnt myself," she said, and didn't seem to want to look at him.

"Let me do it." He moved forward awkwardly. Seeing him shamble that way, she couldn't help smiling. He knocked into the table.

"I can manage," she said. "Really, there isn't room."

Neither one of them said anything for a while. But Sonny could feel himself blushing. He didn't see why he had to blush sometimes.

"I'm sorry about your sister," she said. "Adrian told papa."

The way she said Adrian sounded awful familiar.

Sonny just stared at her. It made her nervous. "Oh stop that," she said.

Sonny got a silly look on his face. "I'm sorry. You're just so pretty," he said.

Molly felt angry with herself. She didn't want anything like that to happen. She could tell what Sonny was like. And she preferred Adrian, she knew that, even if she didn't prefer him quite in the take-it-for-granted way she had two minutes ago.

"It must have been lonely for your sister up there," she said. "We were going to ask her down here for a month or so, and your mother too. It's funny I haven't even met your mother. It was all arranged."

Sonny just looked blank.

Molly put the tray of hot biscuits on the table. With a smile she handed him one, and managed to look him straight in the eye, from very far away. She was a girl who knew how to handle things like that. She also knew how to handle herself. "I thought you knew," she said. "Really, Adrian's the limit. We've been engaged for six months now. Didn't he even tell your mother?"

Yes, he probably had told Annie. For Annie had seemed to take those hunting trips of Adrian's pretty quietly lately for someone who usually worried about her children night and day. But nobody had told Sonny.

"Hunting in the mountains," said Sonny.

Molly looked startled. "What?"

"He always said he was out hunting," said Sonny. He felt as though he'd been slapped.

Molly burst out laughing. "Well, I guess he was, at that, in a way." She hesitated.

"I'm very fond of Adrian. I admire him. He's dependable."

It was more than she'd meant to say. But she was rattled.

Sonny snorted. "Adrian wouldn't care if the world fell down tomorrow. Adrian doesn't care about *anything*."

"He wouldn't let it fall down either," said Molly. And said it sharply. She thought she knew Sonny's type. Whether she did or not, he was behaving like a spoilt child.

"What's that supposed to mean?"

"What it says," she said. And didn't leave Sonny any choice to do anything but exactly what he did do, which was get out of there.

After a while Adrian came in.

"What'd you do to Sonny?" he asked. "He looks funny."

"He didn't know we were getting married."

Brother thought that over for a while. "Oh I see," he said.

"You don't see anything. He's a nice boy."

"He's a damn fool."

Molly smiled. "That doesn't prevent his being a nice boy, does it?"

"Ummm," said Brother, but when they finally got everything on the table, he spent most of his time watching both of them. It made Molly angry, until it occurred to her that probably it was flattering if someone was jealous.

CHAPTER EIGHT

IT WAS EIGHT by the time they got away, but the moon was up, and it was a full moon, the color of skimmed milk in that cold, clear, mountain air, which itself had the dark, sharp slap to it of a root cellar when you go down out of the heat and the light after vegetables or maybe an apple. Come to think of it, that was what this part of the world smelled like, pungent and heavy and earthy, like a winter apple with slightly yellow, watery flesh, but some bite to it all the same.

In the moonlight that land looked richer than ever. The grass flowed like velvet, and that rare and valuable stream running cold over its stones glittered in the moonlight as it rippled along. Behind them the house stood white on its hill, and they rode into the shadow of a clump of oak trees. At home poor Annie couldn't make a tree grow at all. And Sonny didn't have any illusions about who would wind up owning the place at home, either. He felt pretty mad, and because he didn't want to be mad about what he was mad about, which was Brother's way of getting what he wanted and everybody else keep off, he talked.

"No brothers," he said.

"There was Ted."

"Yeah, what happened to Ted?"

"The Indians got him, up near Tucumcari, about six or seven years ago. They don't mention him much."

For Brother, it was a long speech.

"Well, when you marry, you marry well," said Sonny.

"We don't want to talk about it, Sonny."

"You could at least have told me, instead of letting me make a fool of myself."

Brother turned round in the saddle to look at him, grunted, and then ignored him.

"I said we don't talk about it."

"Okay, okay. Someday I'd like to know just what you do talk about, though."

Brother chuckled. "I save my breath," he said. "If we're going to ride all night, we'll need it. And that's what we're going to do."

So Brother being Brother, that's what they did.

It was lonely country through there, and a lonely ride. Even the mountain lions didn't seem to like it much, which made it fine for the deer, but there weren't many deer either, and no houses of any kind. Sometimes Indians went through; Indians will go anywhere except out in the open, so you had to keep a sharp eye out. But Navarro had driven the horses that way all right.

By the time false dawn had come round, they were in the hills above Naco, as far as they could tell. The moon was down by then, and it was hard to see much. Besides, riding all night that way, they were pretty bleary. They didn't have any bedrolls, and the ground wasn't warm enough to attract a snake. So they just lay down where they were and dozed off.

When Sonny woke up, the sun was slanting over him; it must be about seven o'clock, and Brother was lying on his back, not doing anything but staring up at the sky. He'd obviously been awake for some time.

"What the hell are you mooning about?" Sonny got up to his feet. "Why'd you let me sleep?"

"You looked pretty asleep, maybe."

"You want them to get away from us, don't you?"

"They'll keep," said Brother. "Just the same, I could eat something." He looked down towards Naco. It didn't look like much, just a cluster of adobes in the middle of nowhere, like any other Mexican town in these parts.

"Funny place to sell horses," said Sonny.

"It takes a while to sell horses," said Brother. "I said they'd keep."

They rode into the town, if that was what you could call it. There was a cantina. They got chili there, and ranchos huevos, and some whisky. What they didn't get was information.

"Don't seem like they like us much," said Sonny, "does it?"

"They're just scared," said Brother. "How'd you like to have a bunch of bandits on your neck, who're maybe going to come back and slit your throat, if you say anything? Navarro sounds like just the guy to do it, too."

They were both out in the street, by now, belching, because the chili was rancid, as it usually was in those parts. But it sat well, and they'd both been hungry. The street was empty. To look at that street, you wouldn't think anybody had lived in that town for fifty years. There were a few fat little dogs, that was all.

"Well anyhow, they know we're in town," said Sonny. "It sure is populous."

Brother went out into the middle of the street and ambled down it. He didn't seem nervous. Probably he didn't feel nervous. But people must be watching, just the same, and the thought of those eyes made Sonny jumpy.

"Just take it easy and don't start anything," said Brother.

"Who wants to start anything? I just want to be alive when it's all over, that's all."

Brother grunted. "Let's go down to the corral."

"What corral?"

"There'll be something," said Brother, and just went right on walking. By the time they reached the end of the street, Sonny was sweating pretty bad, but sure enough, there was a corral, empty, but used recently. The sun cast hard morning shadows from the stripped poles it was knocked together from, but there wasn't anything else round there to cast any

NAVARRO

shadow. There wasn't any cover anywhere, and that could work both ways.

"Why the hell did you want to walk? They could take the horses by now."

"It inspires confidence," said Brother, and headed for the corral.

It was empty, of course, but the dirt was considerably churned up. Navarro had been there all right, or anyhow, somebody had. Brother squatted down to take a better look.

"Somebody's coming," said Sonny.

Brother straightened up and turned round. "Thought maybe somebody would," he said.

A short, greasy little man in a dirty white singlet and droopy pants was trotting towards them, from the end of the street.

"Alcalde, probably," said Brother, and grinned. "Looks a mite scared, don't he?"

The man came up with some self importance. But it wasn't the sort of importance that was going to carry him very far, you could see that.

"See you had some horses through here," said Brother, giving the man a big grin.

The man looked at the hoof marks as though he couldn't see them and said nothing.

"Quite a few, by the looks of it."

"You can see for yourself, we have no horses, Señor. Not even in the village, do we have any horses."

"Now that's a pity, because we heard maybe here we could buy some horses," said Brother. "Heard it right recent too."

"As you can see for yourself," said the man, and spread his arms. But he'd been looking them over the whole time. He seemed to be trying to make up his mind. And he was scared all right, as well as angry about something.

You could always tell. They got a cunning look on their faces when they were scared.

"Yeah, I see," said Brother. "I wouldn't worry about their coming back none. By the time we get through with them, they won't be doing much riding."

The Alcalde thought that over.

Brother let him do it. But not for too long. "Well, where'd they go?" he asked.

"East."

"Navarro take your horses too?"

"They were here, drinking tequila. We did not want them here. But men like that do not do what we want."

"Last night?"

"They left at dawn."

"That's more like it. Any idea where they're headed?"

The Alcalde shrugged. "They did not say. Perhaps to Chihuahua. Perhaps not."

"Chihuahua's a hundred and fifty miles away."

"Myself, I think they will go to Agua Prieta," said the Alcalde. "It is bigger than here. And if they are taking the horses to Chihuahua, they will want to rest them first."

"They talk like that?"

"Pedro did."

"Who's Pedro?"

"Navarro and he ..." began the Alcalde, and didn't know how to finish it. Besides, by then Brother was headed back towards the street.

"What will you do when you catch up with them?"

Brother had swung up on his horse. "Kill them," he said.

"They are thirteen, besides Navarro."

"It's a sizable number," said Brother, and got out of there.

CHAPTER NINE

Unlike Naco, Aqua Prieta was a sizable town near what is Douglas, Arizona now, out in hot, flat land, but was in the middle of Mexico then, surrounded by those bleak hills that look like the stubble on an unshaved man towards evening. It was only twenty miles from Naco. By taking it not too easy but not too hard either, they made it there by dusk.

But it was livelier than Naco. You could tell that just by the look of it. There were lights burning which seemed brighter as the darkness increased, a good many lights, but somehow, surrounded by those heaving hills, the effect was more lonesome than cheerful. The only business in a place like that was bars, brothels, and cheap cafes. But this being Saturday night, it was a roaring business, by the looks of it.

They both looked at it for a while, before turning down into it. They'd been riding a long time. Just then Sonny didn't feel like catching up with Navarro. If he'd been alone, he could have brooded about it, and that would have gotten him through the first hurdle. If you've never killed anybody, doing it the first time is just as hard as it is to do anything the first time. You have to square yourself off. You have to get ready. And here Brother was not leaving him time to get ready, not to mention watching him all the time.

One thing Sonny wasn't going to do, he wasn't going to show he felt scared.

It didn't take them long to reach the outside of town. Nobody paid any attention to them. It wasn't likely they were expected, anyhow. And besides that, everybody in town seemed to have been drinking since noon, and they weren't exactly in condition to want to ask any questions.

The moon was up and cast long shadows from the adobes. They could hear shouting from somewhere, just a drunk by the sound of it, and Mexican music. Beyond the first few buildings, there was a public corral, which seemed a lot more crowded than it had any right to be.

"We leave the horses here," said Brother.

"You taking over?" asked Sonny.

"Yeah."

To tell the truth, Sonny was relieved. All at once he didn't want to be on his own in this thing. Not just yet, anyway.

There wasn't anybody round the corral, but as soon as Brother swung out of the saddle, there was a small boy under his feet, one of those quiet, determined small boys you always find round towns like this, trying to turn a penny on anything they can find. Business couldn't be too good tonight, because the boy looked discouraged. Adrian gave him two bits to guard the horses. That was a fortune, apparently. The boy said he would guard them well.

Said it to blank air and Sonny. Brother had disappeared among the horses, leaving Sonny to talk to the boy, who seemed to admire him, which made Sonny feel better. He'd nothing against the admiration of small boys. It was cold in the corral. And the night seemed full of waiting. He could hear the rattle and clink of Brother's spurs as he moved among the horses. Brother was good with horses. They stirred, but they didn't shy, and they didn't make any noise. Then he was back again.

"Cunningham's all right. One of them, anyhow," said Brother, and gave a sidewise smile. "So this is it, I guess. Let's get going."

"What about the rifles?" Sonny felt a lot safer with his rifle.

"Leave 'em."

"How do we find them?"

"We just find them. I don't guess it matters much how," said Brother, and moved quietly back into the shadows. Sonny hesitated and then followed him.

There were two cantinas in town. The first one they hit didn't look popular, and a glance through the window and they could see it wasn't. There was nobody in there but an old woman and a couple of even older men. It wasn't exactly a lively place. If they hadn't stumbled on it, they wouldn't have known it was there. But finding the other one wasn't any trouble. You just followed the music and the racket, like a bad smell, until you found out where it came from.

It was a fancier place, too, with a porch, two windows in front, and a sign over the door. But since they didn't have any way of knowing what was inside, they didn't go in through the door, but slipped sideways, where there was an alley, and then round the back.

There was a tumble-down yard at the back, with everything in it that somebody had wanted to throw out and had been too lazy to cart somewhere else. The shadows were deep, and it was hard to see where they were going, but high up in the back wall was a long, narrow window. Not much light came out of it, but you could see the reflection of lights against the ceiling, inside. There was an old cast-iron stove practically underneath it.

"Okay, boy, hop up and do your stuff," said Brother, and gave him a boost.

Sonny peered into the room. It was a long, narrow, high-ceilinged room, with a bar against one wall, and tables. The place was packed, men mostly, and the kind of cheap tart you find in a place like that.

A man turned round towards the back wall, and Sonny found himself staring at Navarro. He'd recognize that stupid, pig-eyed, pock-marked, greedy moon of a face anywhere. Navarro, by the look of him, was drunker than hell.

Sonny got out one of his .44s.

"You damn fool, get down off of there."

Sonny didn't pay any attention. He just wanted to shoot, that was all.

Brother reached up and knocked the gun out of his hand. It fell against the stove and bounced down onto the dirt. It made a hell of a lot of noise, but nobody seemed to notice. Sonny jumped down after it.

"What's the big idea?"

"We're two against fourteen or fifteen. What do you think they're going to be doing while you're muzzle-loading that thing?"

Sonny picked up his gun and didn't say anything. But he shoved it back into its holster.

"I take it they're in there," said Brother. "Besides, you'd probably shoot off the head of somebody just trying to buy an honest drink."

"You got any better ideas?"

"Maybe." Brother stood there a moment, and then took out his knife. It was a razor-sharp skinning knife with a big thumb guard, and what light there was glanced off it as he hefted it. He slipped it back into its scabbard. "Let's go round the front," he said.

One thing about knives, they don't make any noise. They moved round the front. Some people came by. Brother ducked back into shadow, and when they'd passed took a look around.

Opposite the cantina was what looked to be a store. Then there was not exactly a vacant lot, because the buildings looked as though they'd been built Indian fashion, anywhere the builder chose, but a dark patch of sand and sagebrush and scrub, before the next building.

"Even bandits gotta pee," said Brother, and moved over there. Sonny followed him. From the smell, you could tell Brother was right. They looked around a while, and then crouched down in the shrubs.

It was a long wait. Half an hour maybe. Sonny's calves went to sleep, and he tried to shift without making any noise. The door of the cantina was a double-swing bar door, and the light came out of the top and the bottom of it, casting an "H" shaped shadow over the porch and halfway across what passed for a street. The crossbar of the shadow was big, the light patches long and narrow. You couldn't see inside. They were too far away and too low down. That monotonous guitar music came out of there, and the sound of a woman singing very badly, but nothing else did.

Then, at last, the doors creaked open, and a man stood on the porch.

"That one?" whispered Brother.

Sonny nodded, realized Brother couldn't see him, and said yes. He didn't know whether it was one of them or not, but he was tired squatting there. Besides, it probably was.

The man was wearing dirty white pants and a dark shirt. He had a sugar-loaf sombrero on. His feet were bare. He staggered off the porch and came across the street, weaving some, but not much. At first it looked as though he might not make it. He hesitated against the store opposite, and then came on towards them, into the vacant lot. You could smell the liquor on him. He almost fell over them, and then, turning his back, started to pee.

That was his hard luck. Before Sonny could move, Brother loomed up, grabbed the man's sombrero, so that the strings of it caught against his chin, jerked his head back, and with his right hand, drew the skinning knife exactly across his neck, as matter of factly as though he were straddling a sheep, or a pig.

The blood came out with a spurt, but none of it got on Brother. As soon as he'd slit, he let go and stepped right back. He'd had his knee in the man's back, and shoved as he got out of the way. The man went down like an old suit of clothes. There hadn't been any sound.

Sonny felt sick. He'd never seen anything like that before.

Brother stooped down, wiped his knife on the man's shirt, and grabbed a leg. "Stop woolgathering. Help me pull him back," he whispered.

Sonny got up, and they pulled the bandit back farther into the sagebrush, where he wouldn't bother anybody.

"That's one down," said Brother, and went back to where they'd been before. His voice didn't express any emotion one way or the other.

"The next one's yours."

Sonny didn't say anything.

Brother made a funny noise that could have meant anything, but didn't say anything either.

They didn't have long to wait. Another bandit was out of that place before you knew it. Probably they'd started drinking at the same time and had the same capacity. This one turned back towards the cantina, so the light caught him in the face. Sonny recognized him. He was one of the ones who had been at the pool. But somehow that didn't help any. With his heart in his mouth, Sonny watched this one come across the street, like his own future walking towards him. He didn't want to kill anybody. That is, he did and he didn't. He shifted his knife in his hand.

This one didn't look so drunk. He also looked a lot stronger.

But Brother was there, watching him. The man was making a beeline straight for them. He stood practically in front of Sonny, fumbling with his fly. That way Sonny couldn't pull Brother's trick. Besides, he couldn't force himself to do it yet.

The man had almost stopped peeing. It was now or never. So Sonny stood up and rammed the knife right into the man, about where he thought the heart would be, and twisted it hard. The man gave a whistling grunt, his hands were against Sonny, they turned, but they didn't twist much. The man's knees came against him, and knocked him over. Then he had a corpse on top of him, and his own vest and shirt were wet and sticky. Sonny scrambled aside, and pulled the knife out. He didn't like that blood on his shirt. He wanted to wash it out.

But he'd done it. The next one wouldn't be so bad.

Whatever Brother was thinking, he didn't say anything. Together they dragged the man back beside the first one. Despite himself, Sonny leaned over and vomited. Not that he had much to vomit, but somehow that made it sound even worse. He didn't want to do anything like that in front of Brother, it made him angry, but he couldn't help it.

"I got blood on my shirt," he said. It was a crazy thing to say.

"Yeah," said Brother. "I guess maybe you did at that." He stood there for a minute. "Come on, let's get out of here. There's no use crowding our luck."

But Sonny wanted to do it again.

"I said come on," said Brother. He bent over and ran for shadow, headed back towards the horses. But he didn't make it. Before they could get down the street, two men and a woman came out of the cantina. Brother slunk back into the shadow of an alley. From there they could watch the three of them coming. The men didn't have much to say, but the woman was talking a blue streak.

"I reckon that's two more," said Brother.

Sonny started forward.

"You damn fool. You want the whole town down on us?"

But Sonny wanted to get even for having vomited, in front of Brother at that. Besides, he couldn't help himself. He wanted more.

As luck would have it, the three Mexicans turned smartly into the alley they were hiding in. So there wasn't any choice anyway. Sonny slit the throat of the man on the left, in no time at all. But he'd misjudged his timing. The one Brother had had to tackle had his knife out and was slashing wildly. The woman screamed and froze. Then she turned and ran back the way the three of them had come, still screaming. Sonny drove his knife into the man's back, but hit bone. It threw the guy enough off balance, so that Brother could finish him off.

Sonny ran, with Brother right behind him. They should have run back into the alley, but the thing to do was get out of there. So they went down the main street.

The woman was still screaming. The cantina was beginning to empty out, with some mighty mad Mexicans. They didn't stop to ask questions either. They just started shooting. Nobody had ever shot at Sonny before. He ducked low, and dodged, and hoped for the best.

They made it to the corral. But they only just made it. As far as Sonny could tell he wasn't shot. But he was out of breath and scared. He headed for his horse. Sitting on top of the horse was the Mexican boy, looking startled. Maybe he'd been playing cowboy.

Brother streaked by him, headed for the Cunningham horses. "Help me, you damn fool," he shouted, slashed their reins, and slapped them on the hindquarters. "Stampede them."

Sonny got out his revolver and shot. The horses narrowed down to the corral opening and then poured out into the street. That stopped the Mexicans for a minute or two. Sonny swung the boy down from the saddle and got up himself, and then they both got out of there, spurring the horses over the back of the corral, which wasn't a high one, but no more than a continuous hitching post. One thing about that country, at night you could get lost in it awful fast. Besides, though they could still hear a lot of noise from town, nobody seemed to be doing anything about following them.

Brother drew rein and got down. He held out his arm.

"Do something about this, will you?" he said. One of those last Mexicans had slashed his arm. It was still bleeding more than it should. Sonny bound it up.

"Well, we got four," said Brother. "That leaves eleven to go."

"We didn't get Navarro."

"We'll get him," said Brother.

"Think they'll follow us?"

Brother shrugged. "They don't even know who we are. These bandits, if they can't prey on anybody else, they'll prey on each other. They'll probably just think it was another gang and let it go at that. I don't imagine Navarro is exactly crowded with friends. That's all he'll think it is. But I sure hope he lost the horses."

CHAPTER TEN

BROTHER WAS right there. That was all Navarro thought it was. And most of the horses were practically mustangs, they vanished back into the wilderness they'd come from. It was trouble enough just to round up his own mounts, and he was eager to get out of there. But he couldn't do that before dawn.

Sonny could watch them doing it. He and Brother had climbed a hill about a quarter of a mile from town, where there was a little cover, and taken turns to watch. Even if they couldn't see much, they could hear anybody leaving, in that night air.

Sonny's shirt was clotted by now, and his stomach was weak. He sat there alone, while Brother slept as though there were nothing in the world to bother him. He'd never figure Brother out if he lived to be a thousand years. But he did know he didn't want him round his neck any more. He didn't want to be seen by him. He didn't know why. He just didn't.

Sonny's blood was up. What Sonny wanted, right now, was more. Only not with knives. Sonny had found out the sight of blood made him sick, and as soon as they reached water he aimed to wash his shirt. He wouldn't feel clean again until he'd done that.

But he'd enjoyed it. He'd found something he could do. And right then, he wasn't thinking about Sis at all. He was thinking about those other bandits and Navarro, and the look on Navarro's face when he'd caught him there in the weeds, with his pants down.

There wasn't much noise from the town now, but there were still lights burning. As the sky got paler, the lamps got paler too.

Sonny yawned. Navarro's men must have stopped searching. It was boring just sitting there on that knoll, waiting for nothing in particular.

And then, the light was already piled up in the east, a golden glow over the mountains there, and then the sun came up fast, the way it always seems to do. The light brought the colors of that world up like a flood of varnish, until everything glistened so hard you could scarcely see it.

There might be nothing in this country, nothing anywhere at all, the way Annie said, but there was plenty to see, if you looked close and were used to it. Agua Prieta itself, say. It was like all the towns Sonny had ever seen in his life, except that one trip to St. Jo, and he hadn't cared for St. Jo much; it was too big. But here you were big and the towns were small. And that, come to think of it, was the way he liked it. He could see Brother, twenty years from now, sitting fat cat on that ranch, real domestic, Molly would see to that, the rich rancher type, going to the city once a year for a spree, and sitting on all that land, with all those cattle, until he died quietly of old age.

But Sonny didn't want to live that way. He'd never thought about it before, but he liked to live this way. Besides, with somebody like Brother in there ahead of you just waiting to lap up the cream, you didn't have much choice. It was funny, he should have hated Brother. And yet he didn't somehow.

A lot more had happened last night than what they had just done. Getting his knife out, Sonny cleaned it off with sand, until there wasn't a spot on it anywhere. There was just that damn spot on his shirt.

Well, if you came right down to it, that didn't mean much any more, either.

The town below him stood out sharply now, a little collection of dirty boxes, with thin little trails leading into it, from three directions, in the middle of a big, empty flat, and no water anywhere, or so it seemed. But there must be wells.

He saw a movement in the distance, and then saw what it was. Cunningham's horses moving into the Mexican hills, after all, but not quite the way Navarro had figured. Sonny grinned, and just sat there, for another half hour, while he watched little figures, rounding up slightly bigger horses. Those would be Navarro's men, ten of them, and then the big, fat gasbag himself. Naturally he wouldn't round up his own horse. He'd have somebody else to do that.

People like Navarro always had somebody else.

Time went on. The sun wasn't hot yet. It was just pleasant. Sonny sat there and went on watching.

Pretty soon he saw some men gathering on the edge of town, and starting out across all that emptiness, as though it led somewhere. He didn't need binoculars to tell who it was. He turned round and woke Brother up.

"They're leaving," he said.

That got Brother on his feet in no time at all. Below them, at the edge of the village, a band of ten men started out on horseback, slowly and cautiously. The early morning sun cast long shadows behind them. You could pick out Navarro without any trouble. He was fatter than the others and out in front. But he was out of shooting range, and acted as though he knew it. As Sonny and Brother watched, the posse slowly wheeled and, instead of heading towards them, circled the town towards the south, deeper towards Mexico.

"Hell," said Brother, and eyed the hills around the valley.

There wasn't anything they could do about it. There wasn't any cover in these hills, and after last night Navarro wasn't going to be easy about any stranger he could spot round there. They had to wait, that was all.

Down in the village a cock crowed. The sound seemed a long way away. And Brother didn't know this neck of the woods, which would make tracking harder.

Ten men, thought Sonny. They didn't look so much. But any way you looked at them, ten men were too many for one man to handle all at once. Or two men either, for that matter. Which gave him an idea that made him grin, an idea which really appealed to him. Pick them off one by one, until Navarro was alone and scared blue, just the way Sis must have been, except Navarro wouldn't know which way to look for death, or even know, if they kept out of sight, exactly what he was up against. He might even go down on his knees and start to howl. In which case Sonny would kick him in the face first and kill him afterwards, whether Brother was there or not.

He glanced at Brother, but Brother didn't seem to be paying much attention. The bandits took about an hour to move across the valley, a long snake of dust which wriggled and flickered, wound into the hills, and then disappeared.

"Okay," said Brother, "let's get going."

He headed down to the town, for grub, and for once Sonny didn't do anything but follow along behind. He was hungry himself. They found the town quiet but a mite nervous. A knifing or two in that kind of a town didn't cut any ice either way, so nobody asked them anything. They got enough jerky to keep them going, whisky, and supplies. Then they got out of there.

By the time they reached the place Navarro had disappeared into, the gang had a good three hours' start, maybe more. The trail wasn't hard to follow, not at first, but the hills swallowed them up, and they were in Mexico for sure now, as though law and the kind of order they were used to and American territory were a million miles away, and no dragoons to the rescue, not any time. They were on their own, and could only hope they didn't run into the Rurales. The Rurales were there to maintain law and order, but seeing as how they never got paid on time, they were worse than bandits, in their own way, if they once got their hands on you. Off the main trails down here, anything might happen, and usually did. That being the case, they had to go easy.

They were riding through arroyo country, practically bad-lands, so they didn't have any choice but to follow Navarro, since nobody who didn't know his way was likely to get out of there before thirst got him. To save water they drank whisky instead, which in the sun wasn't so wise a thing to do. Hot whisky makes you drunker than hell.

At noon they came to a sort of crossroads, where flash floods had ripped three watercourses, dry now, down to one draw. Everything was piled up there, wood from God knows where, the bones of a dead cow, and broken bottles. But the trail turned northeast, which was a break. Maybe Navarro was headed back to the border after all.

They went uphill, where the channel had dug. real deep, the walls of it towering over them. There was a funny fresh smell in the air, as though there'd been an explosion somewhere; the horses shied, and before they had time to hear it, the wall of water came cresting round the bend, straight at them.

It must have been going forty miles an hour.

Sonny didn't have time to think. On his left there was an indentation in the arroyo wall. He spurred his horse into that. He heard Brother shout behind him, but didn't have time to do anything. The horse screamed and scrambled frantically at the bank. The wall of water went right past, but the backflow slapped the horse against the dirt; it lost its footing, and Sonny felt himself go down and grabbed at anything he could hold. There wasn't anything to hold. He half drowned. Then the ebb of the water caught him as fast as the flow had and smacked him silly against the crumbling bank. He dug into the loosened dirt, knowing that if he couldn't get a hold in it somehow, he was gone for sure. His mouth got full of dirt, and he almost blanked out. Then, as fast as it had come, it was gone and the water wasn't more than a foot of slime and mud, and angry foam around him.

He got up, clawed the muck off him, and looked round. There wasn't any sign of Brother, but the horse was okay, scared, and ready to bolt, but okay. He hobbled over and grabbed the reins, and sloshed down through the mud, leading it. The saddle roll was soaked. The cap had come off the water bottle, and the water inside had turned to mostly sediment. Round a bend, a bend that hadn't been there ten minutes ago, he came on Brother, struggling to get out of about four feet of mud that had piled up against the debris at the meeting of the three channels, and in water up to his chest. The horse was all right too, scratched and bleeding, but no legs broken, thank goodness.

An hour later and you wouldn't know there'd been any flash flood there, except that the ground was damp and there was a puddle or two steaming in the sun. But all traces of the trail were gone, and they'd no way to tell where they were. They could just pray and hope for the best. At one of the puddles Sonny rinsed out the water bottle and put in fresh. Fresh was a third sediment and tasted awful, but that made it two thirds better than nothing. Then they went on following that arroyo for hours, while the sun went down, but what else could they do?

They didn't talk much.

The shadows got deeper.

It was long about evening, when the arroyo got shallower and dribbled out, and they found themselves on the edge of a plain, sheer on every side, except the north, where there was a saddlebag mountain, sheer limestone by the look of it, and not a bush, let alone a house, anywhere. The ground was hard. They couldn't find any traces of Navarro, and low shadows in all that stubble didn't make looking any easier.

The mountain was about a mile off. Brother stared at it.

"Something's moving up there," he said.

And something was, sure enough, up near the top, moving along a long shelf so narrow you couldn't even spot it, just the dark dots moving upward across it towards the saddlebag.

Brother turned in the saddle to look at the sun. They had maybe half an hour of it left. "Let's get moving, and hope they didn't spot us," he said wearily.

Navarro wasn't just quarry now. He was their only way out of there. By the time they reached the foot of the mountain, the sun was down. But there was an afterglow, not that that helped much, and after a while they picked up tracks again and started upward. The mountain was slanted the wrong way. It didn't get any afterglow, and the trail wasn't wider, most places, than two and a half feet. The best they could do was trust the horses. That trip up lasted hours, and sometimes Sonny found his right stirrup hanging over exactly nothing. He looked at the rock wall on his left, and tried not to think about it. But the only thing that got him up there was that there just plain wasn't anywhere else to go.

It was midnight when they reached the saddle, and both so tired out, not to mention the horses, that there wasn't any point in going on. The saddle had some scrub pine not more than three feet tall, any of it, and the horses acted as though there must be water. The sky was full of hard little stars, and the moon was up, but because the crag threw a shadow, you couldn't see much in the saddle itself. So they got down and made dry camp, and let the horses find the water themselves.

The rest made them feel a lot better. So did dry camp, not that you could call anything they had with them exactly dry, except the powder horns, which were corked tight. They divided the jerky; nothing but days of soaking will make jerky soft, but it helped some. The night was as cold as the day had been hot. They were both shaking with chill, and the blankets were dry outside, but inside wet as soaked bread. So Sonny walked around.

He hadn't been over to the far side of the saddle so far. So he went over there. The drop on the other side was gradual, the little, squat scrub pines stood around like small gray ghosts, and there was a wind blowing. The country just rolled away from the saddle as far as you could see, as though it were tired, until it lapped vague rows of hills against the horizon.

He jerked to attention. Somewhere out there, something had caught his eye. It took him a while to spot it again. But there it was, a tiny, red, dancing glow that came and went and disappeared if you looked at it hard, but it was there all right.

He went back to Brother.

"They're down there. I spotted a fire."

"Could be anybody."

"It's them," said Sonny.

Brother didn't question that. He yawned. "How far?"

"Hard to say. Three or four miles maybe."

Brother lay down and put his head on the driest part of his blanket roll.

"Well?"

"Sleep on it."

"You make me sick. You want them to get away?"

"I said sleep on it. I didn't say sleep for the rest of your life," said Brother, and turned over.

At that, he was the one who got Sonny up, not the other way round. Sonny had gone out like a light, as soon as he hit the ground.

Brother had to shake him pretty hard and jerk him up by his shirt to get him walking. Sonny felt himself being walked round, but it wasn't until he saw the sky was green that he realized they had to get going. Over his head Venus was just beginning to fade out of the sky.

The fire was out by the time they got to the place from which he'd seen it, but Sonny had marked it down pretty well, and the cold air had gotten him awake. They jogged on for an hour into the thinning darkness. The moon was still up. Those scrub pine sat there on the hillside, like people in ambush.

The land was richer up here than it had been down below. The water table must be higher, or else there were hidden springs. In the crotch of the next hill, they came on a stand of real trees, real cottonwoods anyhow, and a thin little dribble of water over sharp stones. Brother let the horses drink and looked around for hoof marks. After a while he found them. After that there wasn't any question of riding much farther. Even the creak of saddle leather would sound pretty loud on that frozen air.

They rode another half mile, left the horses, and went on ahead on foot. It was subalpine country, which gave them plenty of cover. The pines smelt like a stone burial vault in that predawn light. It was maybe forty-five minutes until dawn. Which meant that if they were going to take the gang by surprise they'd have to move fast.

The land took a dip ahead of them. There must be a stream in between in the spring, though it was dry now. On the opposite bank they could see the whole damn outfit, and not a sentry posted anywhere. Together they studied the layout. Above the camp was a spur of rock, maybe fifty feet high.

Shooting from up there, they'd have an advantage. But they'd need the horses. They went back the way they came, unpacked the powder horns, and divided their powder.

"Hell," said Brother, and shook out one of the horns. When he'd been carried down and smashed against the logs by the flash flood, the bottom of the horn had been staved in. The powder in it had dribbled away. He reached for the other horn. That one was okay. But with the powder in it divided up, it didn't leave them enough charges to get more than a couple of them. Still, a couple would help. They muzzle-loaded the rifles and got out of there as quietly as they could, leading the horses down through the gully about a hundred yards north of the camp and up the hillside towards the rock.

Navarro stirred and woke up. He hadn't heard anything, he certainly didn't see anything now, but something had waked him up. When he was a child, if anybody had come within three feet of where he was sleeping, he'd wake up, with a chilly, frightened sensation all over him. That was the way he felt now.

Pedro had said they were safe and to forget it. One man dead he could have forgotten. Four was something else again. He'd felt safe himself, once they were out of Agua Prieta. Nobody could follow them through the badlands, and the flash flood had washed out their trail. But now he felt nervous.

He squinted round him and listened. He didn't hear anything. Just the same he had the idea that there was something out there. This country had its own ghosts, and while Navarro didn't believe in ghosts, he didn't believe in being out of doors at night either. The men were asleep. The horses were still. But something was wrong.

He leaned over to wake Pedro and saw that Pedro had been watching him. He didn't like that. Pedro watched him too damn much these days.

"Get up. We gotta get out of here."

Pedro just stared at him. "You are afraid?"

"I'm never afraid."

"You look afraid."

"Get up," said Navarro, and kicked him.

"I am afraid too," said Pedro and got up. "But I think perhaps we are afraid of different things."

Navarro looked over his shoulder. Pedro said nothing about that, but he smiled. Navarro ignored the smile, but that didn't mean he didn't think about it.

Pedro was ambitious and clever. Too clever perhaps. But right now it was important to get the men moving.

Brother and Sonny worked the horses round behind the rock, took down their rifles, and worked their way towards the edge, lying belly down and edging their way the last few feet, until they had their sights on the camp below. It was still too dark to see much, though. Sonny's foot dislodged a dribble of gravel. He caught at it with his hand, before it could go over the edge and drop. He wanted to take them by surprise, wing two or three of them, and then get out of there. That was as far as he'd thought about it.

Then they both heard sounds down below. Sonny couldn't see much. He got up on one knee, and peered down.

"Hell, they're moving out," he said, and felt foolish. It wouldn't do any good to shoot now. Standing up, he could see the rump of the last horse, disappearing into the trees. So there went a night's work for nothing.

There was nothing to do but trail them along the ridge.

"Better ride a hundred yards ahead. Then if they shoot one of us, the other'll be left to finish the job," said Brother.

"Yeah, and who rides ahead?"

"I do, Sonny boy," said Brother, and kneed his horse ahead.

So most of the morning they rode, down out of that low sierra, after a while, into land with less cover, the bandits ahead of them heading north, always north, which, now that the country was beginning to look familiar again, meant they were headed one place, and one place only, Juarez, there not being anywhere else to head in that direction in those days.

That would probably mean trouble. Juarez isn't exactly a beauty spot even nowadays, let alone what it was then. It was not exactly a town that had a welcome sign out across the main thoroughfare.

But then, by this time, trouble was about what Sonny was after, though maybe he didn't know it exactly yet.

CHAPTER ELEVEN

CUIDAD JUAREZ didn't even have a thoroughfare. It was a random town, on the other side of the Rio Grande from El Paso and therefore Texas, which in those days wasn't rich the way it is now but was just as big, and when you met someone from Texas, you usually knew who it was you were meeting.

Getting there had been a ride of two hundred miles, most of it through dry mountains, the Perilla, through Black Draw, and into Guadelupe. It was also Apache country, and had been since the uprisings late in the seventeenth century, when the missionaries got spitted and fried and the big adobe and rubble churches were left to the desert foxes once their roofs fell in.

That Navarro was headed for Juarez was pretty clear, there not being anywhere else to head for in the Mexican states of Sonora and Chihuahua. But he was sure taking his time about getting there. Sonny and Brother followed his trail, up over the San Luis Pass, in the Animas, across the lower end of the Playas Valley where it forked into the Dog Mountains, and through the Alamo Huedos, which were even bigger mountains, but not so friendly. After that the trail seemed less certain, as though maybe there'd been trouble, until it headed into Mexico again, past a ruin called El Espia and into a sandy plain, whirling with go-devils, where they had to lag a good while behind if they didn't want to be spotted. This was cactus country. The Joshua trees stood with their arms up, like a crowd turning to watch the sun from a hill. At night Joshua trees aren't exactly friendly things to look at either, and there were a lot of javelina down there in those days, a savage wild pig that will charge anything any time it feels like it. The coyotes were out, and there were other sounds which might be Indians, and then again might not; you could never tell, until they were on top of you, exactly what you were up against. They didn't dare light a fire either. They couldn't know how far ahead of them or how near to them Navarro was camped. So they had to sleep and eat cold.

Next day they came up to the Laguna de Guzman, a big, shallow brackish lake with an island at the north end of it, full of salts, and not much good for anything. But the Rio Casas Grandes curved down into it, and though the bed was dry, by digging round they got enough water in pot holes for themselves and the horses, and to wash the salt off. They'd been in the Lagoon long enough to wash two weeks' dirt off themselves and the salt on.

Then north to Juarez and a hotel, Mexican style, with a patio, a fountain, and the rooms with red tile floors and blue tile walls halfway up. Brother didn't see any reason why they should suffer any more than they had to; and after they'd cleaned up, had a nap, and shoveled in some cooked food for a change, even Sonny had to admit he felt a lot better. Juarez was the biggest town he'd ever seen, a lot bigger than El Paso was in those days, and a lot more permanent.

He said he was going to take a look round.

"Okay. Watch yourself," said Brother, and let it go at that. Maybe he felt like being alone himself.

So Sonny got out of there with a considerable swagger, and went for a stroll, not knowing where he was headed, or just how conspicuous he was, six feet, which is taller than most Mexicans by a long shot, and with that Colt strapped over his groin. The Mexicans didn't exactly like gringos down there, and besides, Sonny looked like trouble. But he didn't even notice. A couple of girls tried to hustle him, but they weren't attractive types, and besides, he was shy and not exactly in the mood. By the time they'd gotten through overdoing the come-on, he was even less in the mood. He wandered down towards the river, which is wide at Juarez and even had some water in it, as far as he could tell in the moonlight, and stared at the lights of El Paso, across the way. He was feeling mighty tired of Mexicans along about then and thought of crossing over, but figured he might have trouble getting back. After standing there a while, not thinking of anything in particular, he headed back for the hotel, but felt thirsty, it being a hot, dry desert night for a change, instead of a cold one, so he turned up the step of the first bar he came across.

And there they were, the whole greasy gang of them. There wasn't any mistaking Navarro, who was drunk, as usual, nor Pedro either, who looked shifty-eyed and sober as a judge. Sonny went over to the bar and had a whiskey. It was all he could do. If he turned right around and left he might be noticed. His hand had gone for his gun automatically. He didn't think anybody had seen that, but he kept out of sight and got back to the hotel fast.

Brother was cleaning the rifles.

"Well, what's eatin' you?" he asked.

"They're here. The whole damn gang of them. At a bar."

"You don't say," said Brother. He got up, stacked the rifle he was cleaning against the wall, with the other one, and strapped on his gun belt, whistling to himself.

"Well, what you waiting for?" he asked.

"Just like that?"

Brother looked amused. "Yeah," he said. "Just like that."

Together they went out through the lobby. And didn't even notice the small kid at the door, who took off as soon as he saw them. They did notice that the fat old woman who took their key seemed relieved to see the last of them for a while. But then she was that kind of woman.

"Friendly-like," said Brother, when they got outside.

"What are you aiming to do?"

"Look the joint over," said Brother, and headed down the street, smack into five Rurales, who appeared out of nowhere.

Not friendly types, either. There's a special greasy little type that goes into the Rurales. Always has and always will. Besides there were five of them, and they were the law this side of the river.

"For Chrissake," said Sonny. But Brother shrugged his shoulders, and trotted right along.

"Nice comfortable little jail," he said, once they were inside it. Well, you could say this for it, it had been whitewashed recently, which was about all they saw of it before they were smacked into the cell row.

"Unbuckle your gun belts."

Brother sighed. "Do as the man says, Sonny," he said, undid his belt, and threw it on the floor.

"Now that wasn't necessary," said Sonny, "you'll just make the man mad."

"It fell out of my hand," said Brother, and went into his cell. It wasn't a particularly clean cell. The jailer slammed the door on both of them, and took away the key. It was a big rusty key.

"Now what?"

"Now we wait."

"Think they know what we're in town for?"

Brother shrugged. "Maybe. More likely they just didn't like our faces. Or maybe they liked our guns."

"You mean they'll keep 'em?"

"These folks have taking ways," said Brother. "Did you ever try to get anything back from a Mex?"

So they waited.

All night, and halfway into the next morning. Then the jailer came and got them out of there, led them back into the first room they'd seen, just about killed himself being obsequious at a door on the right, and told them to go in.

They went in. The whitewash was fresh in here, too. Fresh as paint. And so was the man sitting behind the desk. A short man with an exact little mustache, not more than twenty-five, in a dapper uniform, with the highest polish on his boots Sonny had ever seen anywhere.

"Señor Henshaw, isn't it?" said the man. He didn't stand up, and pretended to read some papers. If you could read in that part of the world, you really were somebody.

"We're both Henshaw."

"Brothers?"

"Yes."

The captain, he was a captain, didn't say anything. He just went on looking at them. Then he put those polished boots up on the table, and looked at the polish on them critically. Then he lit a cheroot that looked as though it had been pulled through a dirty bushing. Brother watched this performance critically, and let Sonny fume to himself for a while. Sonny didn't look any too happy about being on the other side of the desk from the law. But the way Sonny seemed to be developing, that's where he always would be.

"Care to tell us why we were invited here?" asked Brother.

"I can hold you for transporting guns across the border."

"Everybody wears a gun across the border. Nobody's going to keep us in jail for that."

"It will do for the time being."

"And just why do you think you are holding us?"

The man looked at the ceiling. "You have blood on your trousers."

"Maybe I slaughtered a pig."

"Maybe."

It was Brother's turn not to say anything.

The man smiled at them. "You came from the south," he said.

"So what?"

"Some other men also came from the south."

"Navarro?" said Brother.

The Mexican wasn't saying anything. "Perhaps."

"I shouldn't think you'd exactly care whether he was alive or dead. I guess you're here to clean up the town."

"I do not care. I do care where he dies."

"What makes you think he's going to die?"

"Some of his men were killed in Agua Prieta."

"Never heard of the place."

Sonny's voice sounded dusty. "He raped our sister," he said. "She's dead."

"That is a serious offense."

"You goddam well bet it's a serious offense. Why don't you arrest him, then, instead of keeping us here?"

The man waved his hands. "He has killed many men. Men like that kill off each other. If they did not, they would be insupportable."

"Doesn't rape mean anything to you?" shouted Sonny.

"It means a great deal. But... who can prove it. Your sister, you say, is dead?"

"So you're going to let him get away with it?"

"I did not say that. But if you have no proof..."

"She's dead," yelled Sonny. "If you let us out, he'd be dead. Or don't you care about that? You working for him maybe?"

"Shut up, Sonny," said Brother.

The man had stood up from behind the desk. His face had turned purple. It was not the kind of face that looked very nice when it was purple.

Then he seemed to change his mind, and sat down again. "You gringos do not make it any easier for us here," he said. "Some of us like law and order, you might remember that."

"So why don't you let us go?"

"No, I do not think I want to do that just yet," said the man.

"You can't hold us forever."

"I do not even wish to try. But for now, yes, I can hold you. You can get a lawyer if you wish."

"You mean you're going to let him get away?"

"He has already gone," said the man.

"I do wish," said Brother.

"There's a man called Slocum," said the captain. He looked up suddenly. "I do not wish to hold you, you understand. But the charge has been made. When I made it, I thought perhaps you had other plans. This is not a peaceful town. I will send for Mr. Slocum, myself."

He did not say anything more. The jailer came in and took them back to their cells.

It was afternoon before Slocum got there. He was a middle-aged country lawyer, who'd probably been a drunk back East and so been forced out West, but looked sober enough now. He was about forty-five, and had a good, hardbitten, brisk manner.

"I got you out," he said, without looking them over much. "It'll cost you ten bucks. It ain't high."

"It wouldn't be if there was any reason why we was here," Sonny told him.

"Son, that's just why it ain't high. Usually anybody who lands in one of these glorified flophouses for no reason, stays in it for no reason until they take him out and hang him," said Slocum. "Now you shush up and be grateful."

"What about our guns?" asked Sonny.

"Gunslingers," said Slocum, as though that was about what he'd thought of Sonny in the first place.

Sonny asked the jailer for the guns just the same. The jailer wanted to know what guns. "You know damn well what guns," said Sonny.

"Forget it, son! They have," said Slocum. "That's probably why you got flung in here in the first place. I bet you had a right pretty gun."

"It was okay," said Sonny.

"Take my advice, you'll let well enough alone and get yourself a replacement in El Paso," said Slocum.

"We take the man's advice," said Brother.

"Nobody's going to shoot you in broad daylight," said Slocum, "not around a lawyer, anyhow." He took his ten dollars, and left them there. It was clearly just the day's work to him.

The jailer said the captain wanted to see Brother.

"Maybe we need Slocum right back," said Sonny, feeling better out of that cell, but bitter about it all the same.

Brother didn't think so. He ducked into the office, and was back again in less time than it takes to tell.

"What'd he want?"

"Navarro's gone south to Chihuahua. Chihuahua's where he permanently hangs out."

"He told you that?"

"He's okay. He just thought we was somebody else, that's all."

"He lets Navarro get away with rape."

"He's right. We haven't got a case. We can't prove it."

"Sis is dead, ain't she?"

"What you want to do, dig her up and haul the body into court?" snapped Brother.

"Somebody should do something."

"We're doing it," said Brother. "Stop bellyaching. If you want to go strutting round this town like a walking arsenal, go ahead, but it's a wonder they didn't lynch you."

"I wasn't doing nothin'."

"Aw hell, let's go back to the hotel, and see who stole the rifles," said Brother.

For a wonder, the rifles were still there. So was the bill.

Navarro had had twenty-four hours' start. Besides, there wasn't much hurry now. If they couldn't take him on the way, they'd get him after he got there. But it would have helped to know whether or not he knew he was being followed.

CHAPTER TWELVE

NOW HE WAS back in his own neck of the woods, Navarro was feeling himself again, that is, almost. He was worried about the men. The raid into gringo territory had been going fine, until meeting that damn girl had changed their luck. And the men hadn't cared for those four stabbings either. Word was getting round that Navarro had lost his luck. He could count on Pedro, of course. But he didn't trust the others, and he didn't like the way Pedro was behaving either, for that matter. If they hadn't lost the horses, it wouldn't have mattered whether his luck had gotten lost or not.

But now he was worried about that himself. The best thing to do was to get rid of the men, disband them, and round up a new gang. He'd done that before. It wasn't hard. Besides, it didn't matter how you put it, once they saw you scared for your life, they didn't trust you or respect you any more. Well, he'd been afraid before. It didn't mean a thing. You could live forever, if you got the other man first.

But it bothered him. He couldn't figure out who'd taken care of those four men. As far as he knew, and he would know, no other bandit was round that part of the country. And that it was anybody else but a rival gang, never even crossed his head. Well, when he got back to Chihuahua, he'd find out. Chihuahua was a place where he knew his way around. Nobody would be able to touch him there.

The sun was hot. They'd gotten roaring drunk in Juarez and had the morning to sleep it off. He had the men where he could see them. He was in his own country and felt fine. There wasn't another rider on that trail.

And yet all the same, he couldn't help it, from time to time, he just had to twist round in the saddle, to see if somebody wasn't down the trail behind him. And that every time he did, the trail was empty, somehow made that feeling he had of being followed even worse.

He didn't like the way Pedro pretended not to notice, every time he did it, either.

CHAPTER THIRTEEN

GETTING A GUN in El Paso wasn't any trouble. That was what El Paso was in business for, apart from gambling, drinking and cheap women, a stage-coach service, and the United States cavalry in town in between Indian wars.

Sonny took care of the guns. A gun isn't something you want to buy cheap, but they couldn't afford to throw money around either. So he passed up the pearl-handled jobs and bought two 1848 Dragoon Colts, 7½-inch barrels, a little heavy and eight years old, but there wasn't anything wrong with the feel of them. The bill for that came to twenty bucks for both, which was cheap but made a hole in their bank roll. Then he said thank you kindly, and looked round for Brother. Eventually he found him on the boardwalk in front of the stagecoach office, sitting with his feet in the mud, reading a letter and frowning.

"Annie," he said, and handed it over.

"How'd she know we'd be here?" asked Sonny, who felt a lot safer on a long leash than he did on a short one.

"I told her we might be. She just took a chance that's all. She sounds pretty blue."

"She's got Pa."

Brother didn't say anything. They never did talk about Pa. Neither did Annie, to them. But they knew the way things went at home. They should have, they'd lived there all their lives.

Sonny read the letter. Annie had a small, precise, girls' school handwriting, almost square. She didn't say much. Though she had a sharp tongue in her head, when she wanted to use it, she wasn't a writing woman. Everything at Covered Wells was about the same. She'd been over to see the Cunninghams for a few days.

But Sonny could see her standing at that one miserable, glazed window they had in the kitchen, looking towards that grave, with that funny, young look on her face you could catch a glimpse of, sometimes, when she was sad, and wistful, and very far away from Pa, even if Pa was in the same room maybe. He didn't want to remember that look. It always made him feel uncomfortable. Sonny had his own dreams, mostly physical, and they were all ahead of him. He didn't like the idea that Annie wasn't twenty-five or thirty but a woman getting older.

What had Pa been like as a young man, anyway?

Sonny couldn't imagine. He gave it up. But the idea made him restless. It made him feel lost.

"I wrote her," said Brother, "if you want to add something."

"No, I can't think of anything."

"No, I don't suppose you can. She'd appreciate it."

"Just say hello for me," said Sonny. "Annie knows how I feel about things."

"Yeah. But maybe just for once she'd like to hear you say it."

Sonny shifted uneasily. But he didn't say anything. Brother got up and went into the stage office. If he sent the letter on to Fort Tucson, somebody'd pick it up eventually and take it as far as the Cunninghams, anyway. He sealed up the letter, folding it in four, and using some wax the station agent had.

That was when Sonny mentioned the other letter. The other letter was to Molly.

Brother got it out of sight. "Okay," he said, "let's go."

They went outside, into their last look at civilization for a while.

"What'd you say to Molly?"

"None of your damn business. And who said you could call her Molly?"

"She's going to be my sister-in-law, isn't she? Why shouldn't I call her Molly?"

There wasn't any answer to that. But Brother didn't like it. Sonny could tell that.

Jealous probably. That was something he'd never thought about. Brother was just Brother, and a pain in the neck most of the time. Sonny had never thought of him as a man before, with a life of his own.

"Well, what're you looking at?"

"Nothing," said Sonny, feeling outside life again, trying to get in, the way he usually did. But Brother wasn't going to let him in. Not ever. Brother was strictly devoted to keeping people out.

"Then let's get moving," Brother said again, and looked uneasy. For the next half hour he didn't have much to say.

What he'd written to Molly was, "I miss you. I wish I was there. You should have somebody round, but I guess I have to see my kid brother through this thing. He hasn't got the sense God gave flies. We're going to Mexico. But I guess I'll get back in one piece, so don't worry."

Which for Brother was a love letter eight pages long, almost. It made him feel shy to write to her at all. And his big, uneven, scraggly handwriting didn't impress him as being exactly what it should be either. He was always careful with his handwriting when he wrote to Molly.

She went with that big green valley. And here round El Paso, there wasn't anything but ochre dust, sand scarcely held down to the ground with a sage brush or two, and dry heat everywhere.

And something was happening to Sonny. Something he didn't altogether like. That worried him too.

He shrugged his shoulder and rode on.

CHAPTER FOURTEEN

H AVING HAD one brush with the Rurales, they didn't want
another. That meant they couldn't go directly across the
border through Juarez but had to move westward five or six miles
for the Rio Grande and move into Mexico as fast as they could.

It gave Sonny a funny feeling to splash through the Rio
Grande, which was low at that season but had potholes where
you least expected them, and finally admit you were in a foreign
country, where throwing your weight around wasn't going to
help much. He wouldn't have thought about it if they'd made
the crossing in broad daylight; after all, they'd been in Mexican
territory for some time before, but the going through the water
made him feel cut off somehow. They made the crossing at dusk,
after a long, low sunset that made the dust in the air shimmer
orange and angry.

Navarro had a long head start. If they wanted to catch him
before he holed up in Chihuahua, they'd have to ride at night. So
that's what they did, riding at random through the unfamiliar
hills at a steady pace, in a long, low course like one side of a trian-
gle, until, along about morning, they intercepted the main Juarez
to Chihuahua trail. A trail was all it was, because anything that
random couldn't exactly be called a high road.

Most of Navarro's ponies were unshod. That made the track
easier to pick up. But just the same, riding at night that way, they
often lost it. That meant that after dawn, when they didn't know
where the hell they were, and if you've been napping on a horse,
you aren't feeling so wide awake and cheerful anyway, they had

to make a wide lateral search ahead of them before they could pick up the trail again. Navarro didn't seem exactly partial to the main road, whether he still had ten men with him or not.

It wore both of them out.

In the day the sun blistered the hides off them. At night it got cold, and there isn't anything friendly about that desert night. Not when you're overtired and don't dare push the horses too hard, because if anything happened to the horses, you'd really be out there to stagger round half dead on your own two feet, until the sun got you and you really did die.

But there weren't any incidents. They didn't meet anybody, didn't see anybody, there weren't even any cattle, let alone Indians.

It was Indians, mostly, in that country, that you had to watch out for.

The end of the second day, they couldn't go on, they had to sleep. They woke up long before dawn, realizing they'd just lost more time, and the thing to do was push on even harder, which they did. They rode through the predawn twilight, straight into the heat of the day, so hot this time that the desert danced with devils, and they got spots in front of their eyes. At eleven a big, shapeless mass heaved up in the middle of nowhere, and at noon they passed it and saw it was really there, and not a mirage; a big, two-towered roofless baroque church, made out of rubble with its adobe outbuildings collapsing into the desert, like the hindquarters of a coyote with a broken spine. But there might be water there, there must have been water there once, so they turned aside, until, sure enough, inside an angle of the cloister, they found a cement cistern, full of bits of plaster and dead leaves, but at the bottom you could just see the small bubble of a tired spring. They watered their horses and filled their bottles, and then had a look round.

Inside the nave, a couple of the big rook poles still collapsed into it, and a mess of broken roof tile everywhere, they found a dead fire, and marks of pony hooves again.

Brother felt the cinders, and they still had some warmth in them.

"Think it was him?"

"I don't know who else it would be." Brother sighed. "Okay. Let's get it over with. They can't be too far ahead."

Late in the afternoon they saw a considerable cloud of dust ahead of them, the dust of a sizable party.

"Well, that's them," said Brother, and scanned the horizon for cover, hanging well back under some shriveled-up juniper that had been dotting the way now, for the last hour or so.

There was nothing to do now but stalk them gradual-like and wait for dusk. Meanwhile they couldn't move, for fear of being spotted, for an hour or so, which meant staying where they were. Juniper has a funny smell, dusty and pungent, like church incense, and even when it isn't stunted, it doesn't look exactly like anything alive, with its twisted trunk like rope lava, and tight foliage, like lichen on rocks, or something else, half dead, that refuses to give up living.

The cloud of dust disappeared into the distance, the last of it settling down to the ground for good. There being no clouds in the sky, the evening came on slow and green. Somewhere off to their right they heard a cactus wren.

Sonny was in a hurry to get moving. A breeze sprang up and slapped across his face. It made him restless. He wanted to get it over with. He wanted to get moving.

"We'll wait," said Brother. "If they're going to die there, they may as well make themselves comfortable first."

Half an hour later, he said, "You're just itching to go, ain't you?"

"It's a job. I like to finish a job."

"You never finished a job in your life," said Brother. "But okay, let's go."

The color had gone out of the sky pretty fast. Though they were riding not more than four feet apart, they couldn't see each other too well. A big juniper rose up in front of them. Brother went to the left of it, Sonny to the right. It would be silly to turn round, but Sonny was superstitious. He felt suddenly colder, and wondered what kind of death they were riding into, anyhow. It never occurred to him he might die himself. He still felt too young to think about a thing like that. But he didn't like their going on either side of that tree, just the same.

He'd really hated Brother most of the time, but it was funny, he didn't like the idea of his not being round either. He stared ahead, but there wasn't much to see.

Half an hour later, Brother said they'd better get down and lead the horses. That was only common sense, but nobody likes to walk at night in rattler country, and the going was tough. They must be in the middle of a prairie-dog colony to judge by the heaps of earth and the potholes. Every four or five steps Sonny caught his heel in one of them.

There were fluffy silhouettes ahead of them, probably cotton-wood, and that usually meant water. They must be getting close to something. As it was they heard the voices before they saw the fire.

Brother stopped at once, and they both stood there listening.

The wind shifted. They could smell the pungent desert wood burning now, and make out the men, moving back and forth, as though they hadn't an enemy in the world. They were just keeping their voices down, because you do that in the desert night, that's all.

That was when their horses got restless. They must smell the water. They couldn't risk any alarm from that quarter. The only thing to do was get out of there fast, and then lead the horses well out of the smell of water. So they had to track back the way they'd come, a mile and a half, to be on the safe side, and then trudge back again. What with one thing and another that detour took up the best part of a couple of hours. But they couldn't risk the horses' kicking up a racket and bringing ten men out after them.

There was plenty of cover, except for exactly where the bandits were camped, with their horses tethered on the far side of them. The ground had a slight roll to it here. The camp was in the hollow of the roll, the horses a little uphill.

"Now we wait," said Brother, and sat down to do just that.

"They're only eight of them."

Brother shrugged. "Maybe the ninth dropped out somewhere."

"Navarro's there though."

Something about the way he said it made Brother glance at him, but he didn't say anything. They waited.

It was a long wait. The gang must have some pot liquor along. They even had the benefit of one very bad guitar and some drunken singing, for an hour or so.

"Well, they haven't spotted us, anyhow," said Brother, and pulled his hat down over his head, as though he hadn't a worry in the world. Sonny didn't see how he could take it that way. He felt pretty edgy himself.

He took out the Dragoon Colt and fiddled with it. The barrel clicked sharply in that cold air.

"You're just itching to use that thing, aren't you?"

"That's what we're here for."

"Yeah," said Brother quietly, and pulled his hat down again.

Along about midnight the gang started to drop off, rolling up in their blankets. It being that cold, mostly they pulled the blankets over their heads, so they lay there motionless, like a lot of dead bodies after an Indian Raid, when the army wagon comes to tote up the losses.

And that's just exactly what they'd be, if Navarro would just go to sleep.

But Navarro didn't sleep so good these days, apparently. He lay propped up on a saddlebag, talking to Pedro, and every time there was a night noise out of the brush, he'd jerk and pretend not to look over his shoulder.

Sonny could even hear his voice. It was the same slurred, drunken voice he'd heard at Aztec Wells that day, all right, craven and a bully at the same time. Pedro's voice he couldn't hear at all. Pedro was an urgent, quiet talker.

Finally Navarro capsized, out of too much liquor probably, and Pedro stood up and hobbled down towards the fire and threw a length of juniper in. He had a gnarled walk. Throwing the log in threw up a shower of sparks, the wood was dry, flames leaped up, and Sonny could see his face and the shadow of his mustache, not a hundred feet away. Then, with a look towards Navarro, Pedro lay down, rolled himself in his own blanket, but you can tell when a man's asleep unless he's faking, and Pedro wasn't asleep yet, Sonny just plain knew that.

The others were snoring. They sounded like a bunch of bullfrogs round a rain barrel. Then Navarro started to snore, and a while after that you could sense that Pedro had decided it was safe to drop off himself.

Something was going on between those two, all right, though you couldn't exactly tell what.

Sonny turned to Brother, but Brother was already on his feet. Together they crept closer, taking refuge behind a boulder. The boulder was still warm from the heat of the day. Sonny could feel that.

He looked at Brother.

"Cut loose the horses, while I keep them covered," said Brother. "And take off those damn spurs."

Sonny hadn't even noticed them. He bent down to undo them. They were good spurs. He didn't want to lose them. He shoved them into the pocket of his vest, but lost his balance, pressed against the rock, and the rowels went into his chest, just below the nipples. They hadn't pierced the flesh, but the pain made him angry.

Making a wide circuit of the camp, he moved in behind the bandits' horses, softly and gently, and cut the reins that tethered them. The horses didn't do anything. They must be used to movements at night. Just the same it was ticklish work, and Sonny began to sweat.

He cut the last reins and moved away, patting the muzzle of the horse, so it wouldn't follow him, which it seemed to want to do. They were broken down, most of them, and cowed, and they'd been ridden too hard.

On his way back to Brother, he looked up and just about froze. That missing guy wasn't missing at all, but sitting up on a rock, with a rifle across his lap, sound asleep. He'd been posted sentry.

If Sonny shot him, that'd bring the whole gang down on their necks before they were ready. There was nothing to do but edge back into the shadows and hope for the best.

But he sure drew a deep sigh of relief when he was safe back with Brother.

"Yeah, I spotted him," said Brother, and put down his rifle for a minute. "It was what you might call a close thing."

Together they watched the camp. Nobody had waked up. The horses hadn't moved off, but the first rifle fire would stampede them, probably. They did look farther apart than before, probably they wanted to follow the smell of water down to the spring, and if they did that, the bandits would be up anyway.

"Well, it's now or never, I guess," said Brother. "I'll take the sentry. You open up on the others." He laid his rifle along the rock, until its sights were exactly on the guy asleep on his rock. Probably he liked to sleep a lot. Perhaps he wouldn't so much mind not waking up.

They waited a minute.

"Now," said Brother, and eased his finger back.

The shot didn't make the sentry fall off the rock. It just shook him up a bit. Brother had got him between the eyes. He had enough life left to jerk his hand up in front of his face, and that threw the body off balance, so it fell off the rock and fell practically in Navarro's face. It only took a second, but it seemed to take an awful long time.

Sonny got the man closest to the fire, who didn't move at all, threw his rifle away, and got out the Dragoon Colt. Then everything happened at once.

There was an echo in that depression, for some reason or other. That was a lucky break they couldn't have any way of knowing to count on. The two shots multiplied at once, and seemed to come from the rocks beyond the bandits.

Navarro staggered to his feet, yelling his head off, and then ducked down again.

The horses stampeded all right, right towards Brother and Sonny, galloping down the hill, crowding each other, going right through the fire, and kicking the dying logs every which way, in a shower of half-obliterated sparks.

Navarro got behind a rock.

The horses swept left and right of Brother's boulder, but Brother was peppering away by then, so they whirled and ran right back through the camp again.

Instead of firing back, Navarro reached round his rock, and took a careful, deliberate shot, not at the boulder, but at Pedro.

If one of the horses hadn't whirled, Pedro would have been dead. Instead, the horse ran on for half a pace before it keeled over, smack on top of the bonfire.

That made the darkness a lot darker. There was a stench of seared hide, and the horse screamed.

Pedro threw himself down. They heard him yelling for the men to take cover.

Out of Navarro they didn't hear so much as a peep. He didn't fire again either.

Before Pedro had a chance to yell for them to take cover, half the men had already started running. They were running straight at Sonny.

Sonny reared up in front of them with his six-shooter, forgetting about Brother, forgetting about anything, and blazed away. He was a good shot. He got three of them, before the other two parted and ran back the way they'd come.

What got him was the way their bodies jerked when they were hit, the momentum of their dash for safety carrying them right on. It was like hitting rag dolls with buckshot, the way he'd blazed away at one of Sis's old dolls once, when she'd decided it had done something bad, and they'd both decided to toss it up in the air and let it take its chances.

He didn't even realize he was laughing his head off. He just laughed and laughed. He was doing something again. He didn't even realize that he was crying at the same time.

Then Brother was shaking him.

"For Chrissake, you poor damn bastard, let's get out of here," he said.

Sonny was still pumping his gun.

"It's empty," said Brother, and slapped him one across the face. "Now get moving."

Sonny stood there, blinking. The rag dolls were lying on the ground right now. Just the way Sis's doll had. He'd gotten one in the neck, and the head lolled over, just like a rag doll. The way a rag doll always does.

"I said get moving, fast," said Brother, and booted him one in the behind. So Sonny got moving.

Brother didn't say another single solitary word. He just led the way, circling round the camp, and making for the high ground on the other side of it. Together they climbed among the rocks, boosting themselves up a chimney between two of them. They dislodged a little gravel, but not much, and after twenty feet of that, when Sonny's hands were torn and bleeding, pulled themselves out onto the first level of a tall rock and lay full length.

The spurs dug in again. Sonny took them out of his vest, put them back on, and then looked inside his shirt. They'd made a mess out of his chest all right. The little punctures were blue at the edges, and oozing. He rubbed his hand over that thin smear of blood, wiped it on the rock, and then fastened his shirt again.

"You goddamn son of a bitch," said Brother, but he sounded gentle. "Pull yourself together."

Sonny looked up at the pale sky until he didn't want to see it any more, and then closed his eyes. When he opened them, Brother was just staring at him, that's all, just staring. Sonny pretended not to see what was in that look. He closed his eyes again.

There was a predawn breeze. It ruffled his hair. And he lay there motionless, still seeing Sis toss that rag doll up into the air, and himself taking a shot at it, over and over again.

But Sis looked like Molly.

He was hungry and he could remember the smell of that kitchen and the biscuits she had been making and the safe, settled feeling there was in that house. And himself looking at himself in the mirror for that matter.

And then he must have dozed off.

CHAPTER FIFTEEN

WHEN HE WOKE UP, Brother was resting against a boulder loose on the rock, with his head in his hands. He leaned back and shoved his hat up with his forefinger. He looked tired, pale, and leathery, and there was still that funny expression in his eyes.

"They're moving," he said.

Sonny tried to get up.

"Get down, you fool; what can we do in daylight?"

Sonny got down. "How long have I been asleep?"

"You just dozed off. It ain't even dawn yet."

It wasn't, either. But there was light. Not much light, but a little.

Sonny heard a horse whinny.

"They're bringing the horses in," said Brother. "They can see us, better lie low."

They lay low. They could hear the Mexicans cursing down there, but Sonny couldn't recognize any voices. Just as the sun was coming up, they heard the horses clatter off, headed south. Then after a while it was quiet, the way a desert dawn is quiet as the light touches it. The rock they were sitting on got paler, and then brighter. The sunlight came across it, and caught the mica flakes on it, until they began to sparkle.

Sonny was worn out. He felt as though he'd been beaten up, and could scarcely crawl, but would feel better once he got his head under some cold water. He didn't say anything. He felt ashamed of himself.

After half an hour, Brother got up, and they eased themselves back down that chimney, which hurt a lot more going down than it had coming up, what with torn hands and all. The last six feet, they just let themselves jump.

There wasn't anybody around, nobody at all, but looking up, Sonny saw a black object floating in the sky and slowly letting itself down to within peering distance. There's no mistaking that motion. That's the way a buzzard always moves.

So they hadn't bothered to bury their dead, probably. They came to the spring first, if you could call anything that didn't bubble, but just welled up scarcely at all, a spring.

Sonny lay down full length, his boots covered with dust, and put his head right into the water. The spring wasn't more than two feet across, and so shallow he couldn't get all his head in. He lay there with his eyes open, staring at the out-of-focus gravel on the bottom, his hair sticky with dirt and now water, and turned his face from one side to the other, so he could get his whole head wet. He could have lain there forever, and his whole body ached. It was so clear under water, and he began to feel calmer.

He took his head out, sloshed some water round on the spur wounds with his hand, rinsed his hands, cupped them, and took a drink of water. The water must be alkaline. It stung the spur scars. But it tasted wonderful. Then he stood up.

Brother didn't look so good. He didn't say anything. Just took his own turn at the spring.

Why did Brother have to look that way? What did Brother have that he hadn't got? Sonny didn't know. But he didn't resent him any more. He just felt he was traveling with a stranger, that was all, a leathery stranger you couldn't stand except when you needed him.

That's what you hated about him, that he knew you'd need him, didn't say a thing, and would be there when you did. You never knew whether he wanted to be or not.

It was pretty galling. But right then Sonny didn't feel galled. He felt scared. Scared of himself, he guessed, or something inside himself that had gotten out somehow.

Like a rag doll.

"It helps," said Brother, and wiped the wet off his face, and got out his gun. "I guess maybe it's time we took a look."

They'd both been putting that off.

The camp was uphill from the spring. It was so quiet that clear, cold morning, you could hear your own spurs catch in the sand.

You can tell when somebody's dead. The air has the same flannel hush to it a city street has on a holiday. It isn't that anything's going on, it's just that you're aware that something has stopped.

But who was dead, and how many, and whether someone might not be waiting with a gun, that was something they couldn't know. So they walked up to the camp warily, taking cover behind that boulder they'd started out from the night before.

It didn't seem the same piece of ground. Daylight had made it considerably cleaner. Nothing moved, except for a wisp of smoke from the scattered coals of the campfire. The ground was churned up, the bushes broken where the horses had been stampeded. There was nothing there but the dead horse, with flies at it already, and five bodies, lying round like heaps of old clothes.

"I guess it's safe," said Brother, stepped out from behind the rock, still with his gun out, just in case, and moseyed round.

Sonny didn't move.

"Well, what're you waiting for?"

What Sonny was waiting for was that he didn't much like the sight of dead bodies. Killing them was one thing, but once they were dead, they scared him. They always looked as though they were going to sit up and look at you, face shot away or not. And that shifting, merciless morning light flooding over them didn't make the illusion any the less.

He came out from behind his rock and took a good look. He couldn't know what his face looked like. He just stood there.

Brother came back. "Nobody round. I guess they lit out," he said. "Well, we got five of them."

Sonny reached out with his boot, and tried to kick one of the bodies over. It didn't seem to want to turn over on its back, so he toed it harder.

"What the hell are you doing that for?"

"I want to see what he looks like."

"You know what he looks like. He looks dead."

Sonny went right on, until the body flipped over. Brother was right. It looked dead.

"I thought it might be Navarro."

Brother gave him a hard stare. "You knew damn well it wasn't Navarro. Navarro's hell and gone to Chihuahua by now. Come on, let's get the horses."

They went to get the horses.

CHAPTER SIXTEEN

THAT PARTICULAR morning Annie woke up even earlier than usual. The week after the funeral, she'd fallen asleep as soon as she lay down. Sleep was the only place she had to go. She'd been worn out, and she'd thought the Cunninghams would drive her crazy just with kindness, and Pa with trying to be tender and not knowing how to do it, quite.

Now she was back to the sleeplessness that had plagued her since first she saw this big valley, where she guessed she belonged now, since she'd never be able to get out. Not that Pa wasn't generous and kind, but he was poor, and besides, he liked it here.

He had been a handsome young man when she'd married him. He was still a kind one. She was fond of him. But he had a curious silence around him always, and though she couldn't say she'd married the wrong man, exactly, she had married the wrong life. Not that she minded the toughness of it. She had enough Scots blood in her to chuckle to herself every time she licked a problem on its own terms and gave better than she got, thank you. What she did miss was elegant company. When the children were younger, it hadn't been so bad.

Pa was snoring. Pa would be late for his own funeral, and sleep through the last judgment as well, for the matter of that, which was nice for him. Not that he didn't have the best intentions. But by the time he woke up, everything had been settled, and sometimes, when she felt bitter, she couldn't help but wonder whether that wasn't why he slept so good.

On the other hand it gave her time alone, and she was grateful for time alone, these days.

She always saw to herself in the kitchen, so she wouldn't wake Pa. This morning wasn't any different from any other morning. She washed, buttoned up her dress, and stared at herself in the bit of mirror. She didn't like being older. She used to feel young inside. But now she didn't feel young inside any more; of course she looked older. When your children die or leave home for good, you do.

Then she went outside and squinted at the sun. When people are dead they are dead, and there's nothing you can feel about that, except miss them. But she did look at the new graveyard before feeding the chickens. The chickens were making a lot of racket this morning. She hoped not enough racket to wake Pa up; for a while she wanted to be alone. She went over and fussed with the pine tree. It had taken hold, in the soil she had carted in for it, and one day it was going to a fine tree, full of that solemn joy pine trees do have. But now it was only a baby, with soft pale green needles and tender bark.

She liked babies. She always had.

Usually she watered it at night. The sun still hadn't reached it yet, this morning, so the humus around it was still a little damp, though the sun would steam that off soon enough. She dusted the dirt off her hands and squinted at the hills. They were so empty and so motionless, it was almost as though she could see somebody riding down them, towards the house. If the hills had not been so empty, she would have waved.

And that was what was bothering her. Adrian would come back, of course. But now Sis was gone, she had a feeling she couldn't shake that she'd never see Sonny again, that something awful was going to happen to him, down there, towards Mexico.

Molly woke up with quite a different feeling. She lived a better life in a bigger and better house. But that didn't mean she didn't miss Adrian. He'd said he'd write if he could, but the letter hadn't come yet. And what she was worried about was Sonny.

For she'd recognized something in Sonny, just as soon as he'd shambled into the kitchen. Sonny was one of those grinning, lovable, unloved people who always bring trouble with them, even though that's the last thing in the world they want to do. They just do it because they can't help it. And that's why she was worried about Adrian. Worried sick.

CHAPTER SEVENTEEN

THEY FOUND the horses without any trouble, poor creatures, pegged out there all night without water and nothing much to nibble on. The first thing to do was water them at the spring, not that you could have held them back, without straining at the reins some. So that's what they did.

Then Sonny headed up towards camp.

"Where do you think you're going?"

"I've just got a feeling, that's all."

"Want to look again, is that it?" Brother sounded grim.

"Yeah, that's it."

"Oh, for Pete's sake," said Brother, but he fell in behind, watching Sonny narrowly. The way Sonny was acting up these days didn't please him much. It wouldn't have pleased anybody.

The horses didn't want to go up there. Maybe there was still a little gunpowder in the air. Maybe it was something else. But with a little nudging they went.

Brother drew rein beside the rock. "Well," he said. But he was watching Sonny close.

The camp seemed just the way they'd left it. There wasn't any point in burying them, if their own people weren't going to bury them. Let the buzzards take care of that. The buzzards were circling down already. While they watched, one of them landed, not so much like a bird at all as like a bale of black hay, coasting down a chute and then bumping to the ground until it righted itself. Funny birds. They always like to pretend they're not hungry, thank you, it's just a social call, and then they dig in, all black, with just that little touch of red, like an old woman's neck ribbon, at a tea party.

That was when Sonny began to holler.

"One of them's alive," he said, and hauled out his Colt.

One of them was alive. The one nearest the fire was getting up, or trying to get up, pulling at the sand with his hands.

"You goddam fool," said Brother, and made a grab at him.

But Sonny just brushed his hand aside, and blasted away, sobbing and crying. He emptied the whole damn gun, while the body kicked each time a bullet hit. Sonny jumped off his horse, reloaded as he ran, and emptied the Colt into the body again, still screaming his head off. And as though that wasn't enough, kicked the corpse, while he went on sobbing.

The buzzard turned round from where it was feeding, and then flapped off, not free of the ground, but just hopping. Sonny shot that too.

Since his gun was empty, the buzzard didn't look much as though it cared one way or the other. It just stared.

Brother got down off his horse and knocked Sonny flat.

The buzzard hadn't been disturbed much, maybe it wasn't used to gunfire, but it knew what men moving meant, all right. It got out of there.

When Sonny came to, Brother was sitting watching him, quite a ways away, smoking a Mexican cheroot, which stank up the air considerable, but Brother liked to smoke, and a good cigar was expensive.

Sonny looked over to where the man had been moving.

"Yeah, he's dead now," said Brother, and didn't say anything for a while. He just smoked.

Sonny didn't have much to say either. He lay on his back looking up at that sky so empty that it just had to fall on you; there weren't no clouds to hold it up.

He felt sick. He wanted to be alone.

Brother didn't intend to leave him alone. He took the ciga-
rillo out of his mouth, and stared at the wet brown twist of it.

"You like it, don't you," he said.

Sonny didn't answer.

"I said you like it. You really like giving it to them. It makes
you feel big and safe inside, don't it? You just go on and on at it,
getting bigger and bigger. It must really make you feel mighty
good. Well, this is your first year."

"What the hell is that supposed to mean?"

"The second year you get worried about maybe being shot in
the back. That's what that means."

"You don't understand."

"I didn't exactly calculate on having a killer for a brother,
either."

"I'm no killer."

"You should have seen yourself right then."

"You wanted to get them just the same as me."

"Not twice. Sonny, you're scared. Just plumb scared, that's
all. If it hadn't been this excuse, it'd been another."

Sonny didn't want to think about that. "Jesus Christ," he
said, "I killed her."

"Killed who?"

"Sis."

"You weren't even there."

"You don't know, that's all. You just don't know."

"Maybe I know too damn much."

"You don't know about that."

Brother hesitated. There's a big space between late twenties
and only eighteen. "Okay," he said. "Tell me."

Sonny told him. Brother could sneak off quiet like by himself,
and get Molly, because Brother was the type of man who would
get what was worth having. But Sonny had just had Sis. He didn't
want to think about Sis. Or about how he'd got to feel about her,
now they were both grown up, and all. There were some things

you didn't ever even think about, let alone mention. But the few times he'd hung on to her, he'd felt that thin little body under that overwashed dress.

It had made him shy.

So he never talked about how he felt about things, anything. But he did talk all the rest of it out, now about that whole blameless cloudless day, and being at a loose end, and coming down on the Mexicans at Aztec Wells that way, and having some fun out of them, for no reason at all except he was bored and wanted some fun out of something.

He could see Navarro shambling out of that bush, with his pants down. And despite himself, because he was hysterical maybe, he couldn't help grinning.

He'd probably see Navarro shambling out of that shrub for the rest of his life, much clearer than he could imagine Sis being driven over that cliff.

Though he could remember that too.

He didn't understand it. He hadn't meant her any harm.

When he got through Brother didn't take the chance to speak.

"Well, aren't you going to say anything?"

"Just you poor goddamn pitiful fool," said Brother, and got up heavily. "And maybe we'd better get moving, if we want the rest of them."

"You want the rest of them, the same as me."

"Maybe," said Brother. "Maybe." But he didn't exactly sound convinced.

"You tryin' to lecture me?"

"No," said Brother, "I don't reckon so."

"Don't you think I wish I hadn't done it? Don't you think it drives me crazy?"

"I don't know what drives you crazy," said Brother. "I just know you got there somehow, that's all. Maybe you just came by yourself."

"You've got no call to talk about me that way."

"Not much," said Brother. "Granted."

"Well, why don't you say anything?"

"I've been talking," said Brother. "Let's hit the trail. That is, if they left a trail."

"You don't think much of me, do you?"

Brother shrugged. "We're in it now. So we finish it. If you're satisfied now that everybody's real dead, we'll get moving. Okay?"

So they got moving.

Sonny wanted to go on talking, now he'd started, but Brother didn't seem to want to talk much. "He knows somebody is after him, now," he said. "And this is good country for an ambush. Maybe we'd do better to take it cautious and ride a hundred yards apart. Then maybe he wouldn't take both of us."

So that's what they did. Brother ahead, and Sonny behind. That way there wasn't any call for talking.

But plenty of time for thoughts.

Thoughts weren't exactly what Sonny wanted just then. They only puzzled him. What he preferred was feelings. But all feelings did was puzzle you too, because they hurt.

He went on riding. The sooner they got to Navarro before he got to Chihuahua, the better off they'd both be.

CHAPTER EIGHTEEN

B Y THIS TIME Navarro knew he was being followed, all right, but he didn't know by whom. That rattled him. Besides, he'd been followed before. What he was worried about now was something else.

He felt shaky. He was used to riding down on people and shooting their guts out. He liked that. He didn't like being hunted down himself. He was afraid to die. To die was the last thing he wanted. He believed in hell.

But he had no desire to go there, and he knew the rules. Once you lost control over your own men, one of them shot you, kicked you out of the way, and took over. That was what was making him sweat.

Pedro in particular.

He knew something was in the wind. It had been in the wind since Agua Prieta. And he knew where to look. So when all hell broke out at the bivouac, even though he was half asleep, and the light was bad, he knew who was trying to take over down there.

That confusion was as good a chance as any to get rid of Pedro, and deal with what was going on later. None of the other men had any guts. And Pedro bothered him these days. He was always contradicting. No leader can be contradicted and stay a leader. So Navarro stood up, took a potshot at him, and missed.

Then the horses came stampeding through, and nobody could make any sense out of anything. For all he knew, his own men might be out to get him. He got down behind his rock and waited.

The light was dim, but there was no mistaking the way the shooting came from behind the ambush of that rock; and the horses having scattered the fire, he could see his own men go down. He knew he should do something, but he couldn't. It had happened too suddenly, and it had always taken him a long time to figure anything out. He hugged the ground and said nothing. He just shook. Fear made him sweat. If he lay still he could at least save himself.

"Navarro."

He wasn't going to be tricked that way. That was Pedro's voice. Pedro must have seen him when he rose to shoot. He didn't answer.

Pedro began to holler to the men, telling them to scatter. Then everything was quiet, except for the horses. The shooting stopped.

It was time for Navarro to take over, but he didn't want to go out there and get shot. Pedro was out there somewhere. He stayed where he was.

The silence lasted about half an hour. But you can tell when whatever is out there has gone away. There's a sort of sigh in the air, as though all the tension had gone out of it. But Navarro couldn't be sure.

Below him it was beginning to get a little less dark. Pedro shouted he was going to scout around. It was hard to tell where he was. He didn't make any noise about it. Then, just behind him, Navarro heard footsteps. Pedro had more Indian blood than he had, and walked like one. He screwed round where he was sitting, with his gun out. But he couldn't bring himself to fire. His finger felt swollen in the trigger.

Pedro just stared him down.

But they both knew.

"We'd better round up the men and get out of here," said Pedro, but the look in his eyes was right over Navarro's eyebrows, where the bullet would go, for sure this time. "You never did know what you'd got."

Navarro looked up at the rocks. Anyone with a gun up on the rocks would have him exposed. He didn't want to get up.

"We may as well wait till we get to Chihuahua. We need everybody we've got," said Pedro, shrugged his shoulders, turned his back on Navarro, and called out to the men.

Nobody had ever treated him with that much contempt. But Navarro didn't shoot. He wanted to get out of there.

Instead he followed Pedro down the hill, to where the camp-fire had been and the dead horse was now. The others came in out of the scrub nervously.

"Okay, round up the horses," said Pedro. "And let's get moving."

The men hesitated and looked at Navarro.

"You heard what he said," said Navarro. But his voice didn't have quite the usual authority.

Half an hour later and they were out of there, moving swiftly and cautiously, with their rifles out, as fast as they could, towards Sonora. There was a difference though, this time, to their usual line of march, in fact, two differences. First there was that string of four ponies with empty saddles, which they drove ahead of them. They all had plenty of time to watch those empty saddles, blistered, cracked, not worth the salvage, but empty all right. Navarro's gang had ridden together for a long time, almost a year now. And then, instead of riding ahead, the way he used to do, Navarro was careful to keep alongside of Pedro, as careful as Pedro was not to get ahead.

The men knew something was going on, all right.

But riding that close, there wasn't much they could say.

They rode on all day. That night's camp was brief, and didn't help their nerves any. Two hours' sleep, and both Navarro and Pedro watching each other the whole time, and who knew what was behind them? The next dawn found them halfway across another semi-desert. They reached the other side of it at about eleven. They met nobody and said nothing. The ground ahead of them rose up in a sort of talus, to a crotch between two sloping crumbling rocks.

It was Pedro who turned round. "Look," he said.

You could just see, if you looked close, at the far end of the desert, where they'd come from, two small distinct puffs of dust. You couldn't see any riders, but you could see the dust.

Navarro didn't know what to make of that. But there was high land ahead. He could rally there. Two puffs of dust meant two men. He didn't know which men. But five against two were good odds.

Pedro was for going on.

"In Chihuahua, we'll be safe."

The men didn't know what to say.

But Navarro had seen that uneasy look before. He'd seen it, for one thing, when he'd taken over the gang of the man *he* was second to. He knew this was a showdown, and it wasn't a showdown he could afford to lose.

"We stay," he said. "We lay an ambush for them and get rid of them."

"So far they've gotten rid of us, whoever they are," said Pedro.

Being true, that was too much for Navarro. Seeing the men move uneasily towards Pedro, he raised his gun and shot him. That he missed killing him wasn't his fault. His horse shied. The shot went through Pedro's right shoulder, but the force of it sent him off balance. Taking his rifle by the barrel, Navarro smashed him in the face. Pedro went down in a welter of blood. Navarro jumped down and went on beating his face in.

Nobody tried to save him.

"I don't like traitors," said Navarro. "Drag the body into the bushes, off the trail."

He waited ten seconds.

"I said drag it out there."

They did as they were told. They would now, for a while. The trouble was he wasn't used to figuring out what to tell them.

Pedro had always done that.

But if he hesitated, they'd walk out on him. He didn't trust them. As soon as they came back, he told them to rub out all signs of the body's being pulled away, and when that was done, sent one man ahead with the spare horses, getting them to trample up the ground where Pedro had been shot, and the ground through the pass, so the trail would be obvious. He hated to spare the man, but there wasn't anything else he could do.

He watched the horses disappear through that pass. There was no time to lose.

"Now scatter," he said, "up into those rocks, on either side of the trail. Once they're in the pass, start shooting when I shoot."

He kept a gun on them, until they started, and took the highest outpost on the rocks himself.

Then he settled down to wait.

The sun got hotter and hotter. It shone straight down into that defile and made no shadows, which was all to the good. The mica in the crumbling rocks dazzled you; it was the sort of setup he liked, the only time he'd fight, with all the odds on his side. That way you stayed alive.

Unless, of course, they were more than two men.

From where he stood, he could see beyond the pass, to the country on the far side, with the decoy horses far ahead, just turning into a patch of trees.

Looking back the other way, he saw the two strange horsemen emerge at the foot of the talus, travel-stained and dusty, just two gringo cowboys, as far as he could see. He didn't recognize them. It didn't make any sense.

Their hats hid them. The shorter, older one looked up towards the rocks warily, examined the trail, said something to the other, and then nudged his horse on.

They entered the pass. It was almost a straight pass, and those horses' hoofmarks went right through it, and disappeared over the horizon line at the far end. The older man seemed to relax some.

Navarro wanted to wait until they were well trapped. He wanted to wait until they were right below him. They had already passed Gonzalez, posted behind them.

Then the younger one looked up, shoving his hat back, while sweat poured down his face. So Navarro recognized him, the guy who'd made such a jackass of him that day at Aztec Wells. Then Navarro realized what it was all about. There hadn't been any need to shoot Pedro, then.

But there wasn't time to think about that. There are other Pedros. You can pick them up cheap. But this guy had brought it all on himself, and now Navarro would get his revenge.

They were still riding about fifty yards apart. If they were both to be killed, it would have to be while they were both in the pass. So it was now or never.

Sonny was about twenty feet below him. Navarro stepped out, raised his rifle, got a good bead on the boy, shouted to get his attention, and fired. He wanted that no-good gringo to see who was killing him.

CHAPTER NINETEEN

ONNY COULD move fast as a lizard when he wanted to. That's what saved him, that, and that Mexicans don't move half so fast as they think. They don't shoot so good as they think, either.

He looked up, saw who it was and was on the wrong side of his horse, Indian fashion, before he had time to think about it. He didn't have to worry about warning Brother. The zing of the bullet and Navarro's shout took care of that.

Then Gonzalez started shooting.

Unfortunately they were caught in a cross fire. Brother wasn't hit, but his horse went down under him, in a screaming welter of legs. Brother rolled off the saddle, behind the horse, got away to keep from being crushed, and scrambled for a clump of brush. He opened fire as soon as he got there, peppering the rocks ahead of him. Brother could move fast when he had to, too.

They'd been caught in a part of the pass where it widened out, the scrub was low, but it made good cover, there were boulders, and there was nobody behind them, and no way of getting behind them. Gonzalez like a fool was on the same side of the rocks as Navarro and the other man. So at least they had something to put their back to.

There was a lull, while both sides maneuvered.

Then all the Mexicans opened fire at once.

"Three of them," yelled Brother.

"Where's the other one?"

"Ahead with the horses. That must have been what tricked us."

"I sure pray he is," thought Sonny. And shifted, as bullets started whining into his cover.

Then he took a careful look around him. Navarro was the one he wanted most, but he didn't see any sign of Navarro. What he did see was a puff of telltale smoke up on the rocks behind him.

It was difficult to place. There was just enough wind to move it. He fired ahead of him and waited, watching where the smoke had appeared, to see it again. Meanwhile Brother was keeping things busy down at his end.

It came again.

He just caught the blurred whitish movement of a sombrero, scarcely visible in the rocks. Again he waited, grinning and very patient. It took a little longer to reappear than he thought it would. That almost took him off guard, but not quite. The man had to come out of cover, to aim straight. When at last he did, Sonny got him before he had time to shoot. The bullet knocked him backward, and then forward over the rock, so that a lot more of him was visible than his hat. Just to make sure Sonny shot him again.

He made a very obvious corpse, whoever he was. That must have made Navarro desperate, to judge by the sudden volley that came from somewhere higher up, in the middle of the canyon wall. Well, feeling desperate wasn't going to do him any harm.

Sonny guessed there'd be another lull now, while Navarro figured out whether to cut and run or try to cut them down. But he was wrong. Whoever the other man was, he must be desperate. Anyhow he kept up a steady fire.

Then he must have had to reload or something, he quit.

They were holding their own anyhow.

It was two against two. Look at it how you would, they'd managed to whittle Navarro's gang down considerable. But there should have been another man. That bothered Sonny. He couldn't tell what might be going on up on the rocks behind him.

One to decoy them ahead, by taking the horses on, one dead, two living, and where was the fifth? So he couldn't be too cocksure about things. The fifth being Pedro.

He was thinking that over, when he saw Brother break from cover and head right for him. It was a second before Sonny could get into action with a covering fire. Brother couldn't fire, sprinting that fast, dodging from rock to bush. Navarro and the other man opened simultaneously. The angry little spurts of dust shot up like small geysers all over the place, following Brother so fast, they were bound to catch up.

All Sonny could do was blaze away with both Dragoon Colts, in two places at once, which didn't improve his aim any.

There was a short patch of open ground, with no cover of any kind, between that last boulder and the patch of bush where Sonny was holed up. Sonny had to reload, and it would be his luck that while he was doing it as fast as he could, Brother would try to spurt across the open patch. He'd misjudged when the Mexicans would have to reload.

Before Sonny could get into action again, a bullet must have got Brother, because he staggered, went half down, and then came right on, just to the left of Sonny, took a flying leap into the brush, landed on his belly, scraping his hands, and then scrambled for cover.

"You okay?"

"Just go on shooting," said Brother.

Sonny went right on shooting, but more carefully now.

"Where'd they get you?"

"Calf."

Sonny started to turn.

"Don't turn round. Just keep them busy."

Sonny kept them busy.

"It's pretty bad," said Brother from behind him. "I'm bleeding like a stuck pig. I got to get a bandage on it. Cover me while I get into a better place and do something about it."

Sonny did the best he could. He didn't hear anything more out of Brother. But by backing up, he could see the blood soaked into the ground, and there was a lot of it, in splotches, leading right back into the rocks.

You may not like your kith and kin, but seeing them shot up is another matter. Sonny went on pulling the trigger, until it clicked on nothing at all. A Colt was too short-range now anyhow. Those bandits were being careful for a change.

He'd dragged his rifle along, too. He reached for it, but he couldn't reload fast enough.

It took a while.

Looking up, he saw one of the Mexicans stand to get a better view of where they were. It wasn't Navarro. Which was a disappointment. But from the way he lingered over it, he seemed sure he hadn't been spotted.

Sonny had never reloaded a gun so fast ever. Then he just took his time, moving faster than hell of course, and got that Mexican with no trouble at all, fair and square in the face.

He went right down, but his sombrero came down even farther, bouncing and rolling down the rocks, and settling on the trail with a little tired shimmy to it, as though even it had had enough.

Sonny shouldn't have watched the hat. Not even for a second. While he was doing it, he saw a white blur out of the corner of his eye, and that must be Navarro, scrambling and dodging through the rocks, making a run for it. He couldn't hear him sob, but he was pretty sure he must be sobbing.

Navarro had luck of some kind. He got clean away, before Sonny could reload. Somehow Sonny didn't think he'd be back right soon. There had been something awful final and scared about that fat rump getting out of there.

Despite himself, Sonny grinned, and wiped the sweat off his face. He had powder stains on his hands, and his hands were shaking, just from the continued recoil. He couldn't move for a minute.

That pass had been a pandemonium of echoes, and now it was so still, you could hear the echoes you couldn't even hear any more. After a little excitement like that, you've got to be alone for a second, before you go on to the next thing that has to be done.

Just to be on the safe side, he reloaded the rifle, and then, hefting it, went at a stooped walk, to see how Brother was getting on.

CHAPTER TWENTY

BROTHER WASN'T getting on so good.

He lay on the ground, propped against a boulder, with his right leg raised up higher than he was, so it wouldn't bleed so much. He had a bandage on it now, of torn rags, but the bandage didn't seem to be doing much good. It was wet with the ooze of fresh blood, and he was just staring at it. He hadn't even been able to get his boot off, though he'd managed to cut away his pants below the knee. The jagged edge of the blue denims looked as though it had been sawed through, and a flap hung down, the way a skin flap does before the surgeon sews it in place.

"Get 'em?" he asked.

"Navarro got away while I was reloading."

One thing Sonny was surer of now, in a double way, than he had been before. This time he was going to get Navarro, but good, if it was the last thing he did do.

He went over and took a look. It was bad all right.

"Nothing to cauterize it with," he said. "But water might help."

He walked out in the open this time, down that quiet little deathtrap that had backfired. He felt a lot older than he had half an hour ago. It wasn't just a game any more.

His own horse had strayed on ahead. He'd go after it in a minute. But Brother's horse still lay out there in the middle of nothing. The poor animal wasn't dead yet. He shot it out of its misery, and got the canteen off the saddle. In that sun, the water would be as red-hot as the canteen was, but it was water, just the same. With a glance round, he went back to Brother and went to work.

It must have hurt like hell, but Brother didn't say anything. First Sonny unstripped the bandage, which was sticky and didn't want to come away. The wound was a mess all right, a big jagged tear in the calf that looked deep. He held the wound between his hands, wondering if he could get the bullet out. He couldn't see any sign of it. It had missed the bone, but it was in there deep. At least the damn thing wasn't gushing blood any more, just oozing and jagged. There hadn't been any flies in that pass half an hour ago, but now they were all over the place, and in that climate they both knew what to expect. Sonny doused the wound with water, did the best he could to clean it up a bit, ripped up some more shirt, and put a bandage on.

"It don't help much but it will help some," he said. "Stay here while I take a look round."

"I wasn't figuring on moving just yet."

Sonny sloped off. He was pretty sure the survivors had gotten out as fast as they could get, but it didn't do any harm to reconnoiter. The sun was very warm.

He climbed the bank, up to where he'd dropped the first bandit. He was a very dead bandit all right, but apart from that there wasn't anything interesting about him. Sonny rolled him over and took a look at his face all the same. It wasn't anybody he'd ever seen before. It wasn't anybody anybody was ever going to see again.

There was a funny feeling in the air, as though time had gotten suspended somehow.

He didn't go back down to the bottom again, but ambled across the rocks. He could see Brother down below, not moving much. He could see the dead horse. He couldn't go in a straight line. The easiest way made a jog uphill. At the top, among some good, safe boulders, there were some shells on the ground. Navarro's, probably. He went right on, until he came to the second bandit. The second bandit had been stationed just about at the end of the gap, with a view both ways. Sonny saw his horse lingering just a little way beyond, not doing anything in particular. There was no sign of anything or anybody else. They must be well under cover, somewhere out there.

The second bandit provided a real find. He was just like the first one, only considerably deader looking, but he had a flask of tequila on him. If the stuff hadn't been fermented with human dung, the way local tequila was sometimes, it would be good for the wound. With that high alcohol, it would be good for it anyway. The flask was sort of pretty, a fancy gimmick made out of dirty blue Mexican glass, with silver fittings. Sonny took a swig and then started back to Brother.

By the time he got the bandage off again, doused and swabbed the wound with tequila, which must eat like acid, so Brother's twitching around was understandable, got it as clean as he could, and got a new bandage on, considerable time had passed. That couldn't be helped.

He left Brother there, with the rest of the tequila for any comfort he could get out of it, and went off to get his horse and scout the trail. He felt a lot safer once he was mounted again, but he kept a weather eye out, all the way.

They'd been decoyed all right. All you had to do was follow the trail out into the brush. Nobody was around, but his own horse seemed to scent something. Sonny let her have her head, and came up with a loose pony. It was still sweaty from a saddle, so he figured Navarro and whoever was left had kept the saddles but turned the other horses loose.

The pony didn't like him much. It probably preferred Mexicans. But once he got a rope round its neck, it followed along quietly enough. He led it back to the pass, got Brother up on his own horse, and rode the pony bareback himself.

Then, before they went on, he did some thinking. Brother's wound would need some looking after. With the bullet still in it, anything might happen. Besides this was gangrene weather in gangrene country, and they both knew what that meant. They were about equally distant from Chihuahua and Juarez and El Paso, but when you need medical help, you distinctly hanker after your own kind.

Sonny was feeling sobered up about things.

"Let's go back," he said.

Brother just set his jaw and shook his head.

"You've got to get to a doctor. They've got better doctors back home."

"I'll make out. We've come this far. This time we get him. Besides, I figure I owe him that."

"Yeah, I guess you do," said Sonny.

But he didn't feel right about the idea. Somehow things had started to go wrong.

"Let me go on then."

"Fat lot of chance I'd have of making it back alone."

When Brother's mind was made up, it was made up. They went on.

CHAPTER TWENTY-ONE

EVEN WITH a saddle, Brother couldn't be exactly enjoying himself. There wasn't just the pain, he must be pretty weak, losing all that blood.

There wasn't anything to see, anywhere, except, in the sky behind them, black specks way up in the air. How do buzzards know when their food's ready, anyhow, not that they're in any hurry to come eat it until it's good and rotten? But they start to check up right away.

They decided not to look back.

The pony was hard to manage without a saddle. It was probably hard to manage with one. Mexicans like Guerrero did most of their riding by grace of a nice, big, sharp-burred Spanish bit, and probably the pony didn't respect much of anybody any more, unless it was having its tongue cut to shreds. But the pony was tired and so were they. They jogged on, the best way they could.

There's something empty about that countryside that isn't like the emptiness back home. Back home if the country's empty, it's empty. But here you never had any way of knowing. You could ride along for days, and never meet anybody, not a single solitary living soul. And then, in the middle of nowhere, fifty miles, as far as you know, to the next adobe, you'll find an old man walking along the trail, just as a matter of course, looking fresh as a daisy, and bent on his own affairs, not that he'll tell you or anybody else what his own affairs are. There never is any explanation for that old man.

You always find him out in the flat, though. Never where the country starts to get jagged and hilly. In that country, maybe you won't meet anybody, or maybe you'll have bandits on your neck before you know it.

Bandits or worse.

Neither one of them wanted to think about the worse.

They were getting into mountain country.

They were still worried about ambush, which meant they had to go even more carefully. Then suddenly, in late afternoon, the whole country felt as though something had been sucked out of it, the sky clouded up, with great purple clouds, but that wasn't what bothered them. What bothered them was a special feel the air had to it, of something moving out there, something watching. Brother looked on up ahead. Neither one of them mentioned it, but they both knew what they were thinking.

Head for cover.

But whatever was out there didn't come any closer.

It made them jumpy all the same. They tried to hurry, but Brother couldn't hurry too much. The chance of starting that wound up again just wasn't a risk worth running.

They were up a ways now, with the mountains right in front of them. There was a sudden cold gust in the air, like a snicker you could smell, heat lightning jagged all along the peaks and down into the plain they'd just crossed, and thunder everywhere. It was the worst electrical storm either of them ever had been in, and they were caught in it, before they had a chance to head for cover.

The heavens just opened, like the bottom of a sluice. It was solid water, beating down the ponies' heads and running down their shoulders and over their legs. And it was cold and sticky at the same time.

Flash floods poured down the arroyos, and water started coming at them from the mountains ahead.

The only cover they could find was under some rocks just to the left of the trail. As cover it wasn't much but it was better than nothing. The overhang kept the worst of it off them anyhow.

Brother elected to stay where he was, in the saddle. There wasn't enough ground to sit on, among those rocks, anyhow. Then they heard the sound of horses.

Sonny went to take a look. And there they were, not ten feet away, what they'd thought that funny feel to the air had meant, thirty Apaches, going by in full war paint, what the rain left of it.

They weren't enjoying the storm either. They went right on past. But it wasn't until they were well past that Sonny let his breath out.

If it hadn't been for the rain, they'd have lost their scalps for sure, if not worse. Apaches have some fancy ideas of what people are for, by way of amusement.

CHAPTER TWENTY-TWO

THOSE STORMS never last long, though heaven help you if you get in the way of one. It was over in an hour or so. But by then it was about dark, and Brother was worn out anyhow.

They had a bad night of it, with no dry wood to make a fire, not that they dared make one, with Indians or Navarro in the neighborhood somewhere, consequently not much to eat, and that dry, and none of the tequila left. There was nothing to do but lie on half-wet blankets and listen to what was going on in the darkness out there. Sonny didn't sleep much.

The way he saw this, it was his fault. If Brother wouldn't go back, at least it was up to him to get him to Chihuahua as soon as possible.

Not that Brother said anything. He lay there, pretending to sleep. But along about two, when he really fell asleep, Sonny woke up and heard him groaning. He had a chill even if he didn't have a fever. But there was nothing to do about it; he was better off unconscious than conscious. Just the same Sonny couldn't get back to sleep.

Brother got quieter towards dawn, but woke up almost as soon as the light hit him. He sounded rusty in the throat, but said he felt okay.

There wasn't any reason to linger there. Sonny helped him on his horse. Neither one of them mentioned or looked at the leg. It was better not to.

There was still mud from the storm, and worse than that, the rain had washed the trail out. Everywhere you looked there

wasn't any sign of a trail anywhere. That meant they had to pro-
ceed by dead reckoning, which wasn't easy. They were both used
to finding their way round their own neck of the woods, once you
get the hang of it, it isn't hard, but neither one of them had ever
been down to Chihuahua before, or much wanted to go there, for
the matter of that.

There was no chance of catching up with Navarro now.
They'd have to dig him out of his burrow when they got there,
and could find it.

They just glumly plodded along. Sonny didn't even have the
heart to whistle, and besides, neither one of them had forgotten
that band of Apaches last night.

The day ground on. The sun got fainter, the sky got cloudy.
The clouds just hung there this time. There wasn't any second
storm.

But Brother was getting worse. He had trouble keeping his
seat, and he was beginning to get wild-eyed. He had cold eyes
anyway. With fever in them, they were pretty frightening.

Late in the afternoon they began to run into signs of range
stock, high ground for the cattle to stand on, though there were
no cattle anywhere to be seen yet. The country got a barbered
look to it. They were going to make it, after all. No signs of habita-
tion yet, and not a single solitary soul, though in another hour
they reached what passed for a water hole, with red water from
the mud in it. The grass began to look greener, and they stopped
there to rest.

Brother still maintained he was feeling okay. But he didn't
seem able to move his mouth too good while he tried to say it.

They hoped maybe they'd reach at least some kind of aban-
doned shelter, range like this usually had a few, to work out of in
roundup time, but they didn't find even that. They had to make
dry camp again.

For all they knew they were in the middle of nowhere, though
by the look of it, it was close to something, and at this stage of

the game, whether it was Chihuahua ahead or not, anything or anybody would have been welcome.

Brother's leg hurt so much, he couldn't get down out of the saddle. So Sonny had to help him down, and didn't like the way he was acting at all, fever or no fever. He was acting as though Sonny was his worst enemy.

Which maybe at that he was.

He got Brother settled, and tried to unwind the bandage, and take a look. It was filthy with trail dust, and needed changing anyhow. But Brother wouldn't let him. He said just to leave it be.

It hurt so much he couldn't hold it out straight, and had to lie on his back, with his leg crooked, most of the time. He wasn't delirious now, at least not screaming delirious. But his mind didn't seem to be working so good either.

There was nothing to give him, but some musty water out of the cattle pond, and he couldn't get down any biscuit, which was all they had left.

Sonny was so worn out by then that he dropped right off.

When he woke up, it was morning, and Brother hadn't moved. For a moment Sonny thought maybe he was dead. He looked as though he'd been waiting a long time for Sonny to wake up.

"Smell anything funny?" he asked. He didn't sound feverish. He was having a lucid spell.

Come to think of it, Sonny did. Something sick and sweet.

For a moment he was really scared.

"You'd better take a look," said Brother. Sonny knelt down, cut the knot, and began to unwrap the bandage. It was stiff and dusty and dry, but there was something sticky in it too. Brother didn't say anything. He just waited.

When the last of the bandage was off, the sight wasn't pretty. The skin was white and cracked, and round the wound, bloated up, and yellow. The wound itself was a suppurating mess of bits of congealed blood and bluish-yellow ooze.

And the smell was bad all right.

Sonny looked up.

"Yeah, gangrene," said Brother. "I knew a man once everybody gave up for lost, and you know what he did, he got some rotten fish, and laid them on the wound, and after a while the maggots turned up, and ate the mess away, and he's walking yet. Only we ain't got no rotten fish."

"What're we going to do?"

"I'm telling you this, I'm not going to lose this leg. Just get me to Chihuahua, that's all. You started this damn-fool thing and I'm going to finish it."

Sonny hesitated and looked at his knife.

"I said you started it," yelled Brother. "If I can stand it, you can."

Sonny looked round for a bandage.

"Leave it alone. Maybe the sun will do it some good. It's sure as hell nothing else will. Now get me on that horse."

Sonny got him on, somehow, and was just as glad that Brother rode on the right side of him. That leg wasn't exactly a pretty sight.

They'd no idea how far they had to go. They still didn't meet anybody. And when at last they did, there wasn't much point in asking the way, because it had been a long haul, but they'd made it. Ahead of them, in the distance, they could just see the glint of sun on a white dome, and a couple of those church towers the Mexicans like, all dribbled up at the top, like a runny candle.

"It'll be all right," said Brother. "It's got to be all right." He was getting feverish again.

Sonny didn't feel so good himself.

CHAPTER TWENTY-THREE

CHIHUAHUA'S a real city, bigger than anything in the thousand miles of that West except Monterrey and Hermosilla. It was the biggest city either of them had ever been in, and if that wasn't enough, a Spanish-speaking foreign city, at that.

It had too many streets. You couldn't find what you wanted just by looking round. Besides, there was always the danger that Navarro would spot them, or that somebody might tell him how two Americans had turned up, from the trail north.

Sonny was bewildered, and Brother was in no position to help. This last hour's ride had been too much for him. As Sonny hesitated, he heard church bells, and that gave him an idea. In a country like Mexico, nuns do the nursing, it's one of their better sides, and the thing to do was stop a priest.

So Sonny rode round the streets, slowly, until he saw one, a thin middle-aged man, with what looked like a market basket over his arm.

The Mexicans in the streets had been getting mighty curious about them. It was only ten years since the Mexican War, and General Scott marching his men through Mexico City. There wasn't any love lost, and this far south of the border, an American had to rely on kindness and his own shooting irons.

So Sonny doffed his hat.

The priest spoke a rapid Spanish, but when he saw Brother, he slowed down, enough to make himself plain, and looked frankly curious. Perhaps not many gringos got down his way. At the moment Sonny was mostly worrying about how they were ever going to get back up again.

Yes, there was a hospital. A doctor could be found. It was this way.

And as happens in Spanish towns, in Mexican towns where folks are bored, not just the priest led him to the hospital, but a whole wedge of gutter urchins and idle helpers ran along beside the horses, to pace them out to the hospital. Maybe all they wanted to do was be helpful. But the trip got to be a procession, and that made Sonny nervous.

Brother was in a bad way, he could see that.

But if they got all this publicity, they'd be where Navarro could get at them for sure.

Fortunately, it being siesta time, the streets were quietly empty. But not everybody in this world spends his siesta time having a snooze.

About twenty minutes of that, and they got to the hospital, a big building, absolutely nothing to look at from the street but a blank wall, with a big gap in it, and a lot of fancy stone work on either side.

But inside it was cool, real cool, with a courtyard, and a fountain. It was a moment of peace in all that wild hunt after revenge. Sonny didn't feel comfortable with priests ever, but he was grateful, and gave the man what cash he had to spare. It was the best he could do.

Then it was a matter of getting Brother down off that horse, and inside somehow.

Some of the kids must have run ahead, for there was a man there, probably the porter, to help Brother down from his horse. He was too worn out to walk. Sonny and the porter got him inside, and there the nuns took over.

Brother passed out as soon as he was laid in the bed. Sonny just sat there, on an old cane-backed chair, and waited. They were a long way from anywhere. And though he spoke enough

Spanish to get along, someone who spoke American would have been a godsend.

He guessed these people meant well, but for all the help that was, he might be on the other side of a wall.

The doctor, when he came in, was a short, sallow man of about fifty. Maybe he knew his business. Who could tell? Sonny sure hoped he did. But how could you be sure?

His name was Coello. He did seem a different breed from most of the Mexicans Sonny was used to, thinner and quicker.

What he thought of Americans who wandered in in the middle of Chihuahua with a gunshot wound in the leg, he didn't say, but Sonny explained how it had happened.

If the doctor had heard of Navarro, he didn't say anything, but his face tightened up. He went over to the bed, lifted Brother's eyelids, and felt his pulse. Brother groaned and shifted around some.

Dr. Coello began to take off the bandage. He didn't seem to like what he saw. He had the bedside manner all right, but like most doctors, he also had some facial expressions that said a lot more and different than the bedside manner did.

Brother tossed and began to murmur. The word Molly came out clearly, and also, "that damn fool."

"Molly," said Brother. And so said a lot he'd never have let out of the bag any other time.

A nun had come in, carrying a tray of instruments. Sonny tried not to look at them.

"You going to cut his leg off?"

"We'll see," said Dr. Coello. He looked at Sonny curiously. "I don't want to give him anything. It won't hurt him much. Can you hold him, just in case it does?"

The nun moved forward with the tray. Sonny went to the head of the bed, and did as he was told. It was a huge, empty room, with a high ceiling, and hard green light from the garden. The walls were painted blue to a height of about two and half feet.

He held Brother's shoulders. You couldn't tell whether Brother was conscious or not. But his flesh felt hot under his shirt, his face was a funny color, and the leg was swollen and looked terrible.

The nun put the tray down and prepared to hold his feet, in case they jerked. She was a middle-aged nun and, like a lot of them, wore steel spectacles. Her face was unreal, but there was a look in it Sonny didn't want to see.

Brother was a big man. A fine figure of a man. And he wanted Molly. Well, Sonny would get him back to Molly somehow. Anything else he didn't want to think about.

The bandages were off now. The doctor threw them into a basket and washed his hands in a basin of water. Then he sighed, held the wound apart with surprisingly hard, bony fingers, and probed for the bullet.

Brother jerked.

The next ten minutes were silent, except for an occasional noise out of Brother. Sonny couldn't keep his eyes away, and trusted the doctor a lot more now he watched him work. When it was through, the doctor bandaged up the leg, and washed his hands, this time even more carefully. He gave the nurse a look which seemed to say just one thing, and then looked at Brother. Apparently Brother was unconscious. Then he beckoned Sonny out into the hall.

For a minute neither one of them said anything.

"Well, does it have to come off?" asked Sonny, who wanted to force the worst, rather than not face it, which was his way.

No doctor ever likes to tell the truth when it's bad.

"There's a chance. It depends how far the gangrene has gone. You must understand that..."

"I said does it have to come off?"

Dr. Coello looked at the nun, who for some reason or other smiled.

"We'll wait until morning. But I'm afraid ... yes."

He'd known it as soon as he'd seen the leg. But that wasn't the same as being told it.

The doctor hesitated.

"If you want to stay here, there's a room down the hall you can use," said Dr. Coello.

"That's mighty kind of you," said Sonny. And meant it. "But if you could move a cot in or something. I'd like to be with him."

Again there was just a shade of hesitation. But yes, that could be done.

And was done.

In another part of town, in a dive called El Chico, which was his usual cantina, Navarro was getting drunk and waiting round for Garcias. Garcias was the one member of his gang left, and when Garcias was going to turn and run Navarro didn't know. Except that the last man from the old gang is sometimes second in command in the new one, and as far as he knew, Garcias didn't have any other offers.

Navarro was feeling a lot better. He'd had bad luck, but now he was back on his home ground that didn't count for so much. The thing to do now was to round up a new gang. That's one thing he'd sent Garcias out to look around for, any guns who were out of work.

So when Garcias came in, and said two gringos had come into town, Navarro wasn't exactly too worried. Gringos came into town all the time. But it made him thoughtful. He at least wanted to know who they were.

Garcias said he didn't know who they were. He'd just seen them come in, that was all, and then a crowd had collected.

Navarro thought that over. "Better go find out," he said.

It didn't do any harm to make sure.

CHAPTER TWENTY-FOUR

For Sonny it was a long night. He couldn't sleep. Not for a long time.

Not until he couldn't stand being awake with his thoughts any more.

The hospital was in a convent, a big, square, seventeenth-century building, with that courtyard outside. The walls were thick. The corridors were shadowy. The nuns who were on night duty in the hospital part of it wore leather heels, which made a frightening noise on the red tile floors. Somewhere in this building somebody was probably dying. Sonny didn't like being shut in that way. And Brother just couldn't die.

And yet maybe it might be better if he did.

He was delirious. He didn't even know Sonny was there. What he said didn't make any sense, unless you'd known him a long time. But it made a series of pictures, and it meant something. It wasn't anything Brother would have said in his right mind. But maybe it was something he would have thought.

Outside in the courtyard there wasn't a fountain exactly, but a pipe in the middle of the place. It splashed. It just went on splashing. And there was some kind of heavy Mexican shrub out there, whose scent got mixed up with the stench of Brother's leg, and that Sonny never would forget. A big shrub with red flowers of some kind.

No, he couldn't sleep.

He felt as though he'd lost his grip on everything, and since he never had felt attached to anything much, or anyhow to any place, that made him feel real bad.

Because Brother was blaming him.

"Why did that young idiot…Molly, I'll be back…oh in a week or two. It's just that blamed young idiot. Somebody has to take care of him. Miss Molly, well, I'm glad to meet you…Oh now Annie, she's a nice girl. You'll like her…And after we get the ranch going…And I won't lose it. I can't go back there. Molly, you can't marry a man with one leg. Why, you're a girl. You're such a purty girl…"

And a lot of stuff Sonny didn't want to hear. A lot of stuff he knew nobody would say to him, or he to anybody. A lot of stuff…

"And that goddam fool has to get me into this. Well that can I do? Somebody has to take care of him."

He didn't want to hear any more. He didn't want to hear anything. He didn't want to be to blame for anything.

And about midnight, to judge by the church bells and the stillness, a nun came in, looked at Sonny's cot curiously (he pretended to be asleep), and left a jug of water, as though that would help.

And later, Dr. Coello. Sonny still pretended to be asleep. But he watched all the same.

Dr. Coello looked at the leg, and at Brother, beaded with sweat and unshaved the way he was, and his face, when he turned to leave the room, was all hooded up, but sorry just the same.

And the fountain went on splashing.

Brother sat up in bed.

"You here, Sonny?"

"Yes," said Sonny softly, and with something dry in his throat.

"They're not going to cut off my leg. You'd like that, wouldn't you? You think I can hobble back there and ask her to marry me, with one leg? You think that?"

"No."

But Brother didn't hear him.

"Oh, she liked you. She's eight years younger than me. You'd do fine there, you would. And you'd like that, wouldn't you? I could see you there, in the kitchen, just eating her up. You think she'd want me? I'm almost an old man. An old man, by her standards. And what the hell would you do when you did get her? You think you'd know how to treat a real lady like that?"

Sonny didn't say a thing.

So that's what Brother had been thinking. He'd been fooled. He'd thought maybe Brother had come to. But it was just the delirium again.

"Why didn't you cut it off yourself? You think I wanted to keep you from wetting your pants? You think I'd ever go back there on one leg? I'd rather die. Oh sure, she'd just swallow and say, it doesn't make any difference. But you think I wouldn't know the difference it made? And you hanging around all the time."

Brother sat up, and Sonny didn't dare get up and go near him.

"You're not going to do it," shouted Brother. "Nobody's going to cut off my leg. I'd rather die first. I'd rather die."

He was shouting pretty loud. A nun came in, and got him to lie down.

And after that there wasn't anything but breathing.

And sleep. At last, the slow breathing of sleep.

Sonny hadn't undressed, not even his boots. He got up, and went out into the corridor, which was empty, and out into the night of the courtyard. And when he was sure he was alone, he just leaned up against the wall, and he couldn't help it, he wept.

He'd hated Adrian all his life. And now he'd caused all this. So he wept, all by himself, getting what comfort he could off of the whitewash that came off on his face.

And then washed his face in the fountain, and got over it, and went back, and lay down, and after a while he dozed off.

When he woke up, Dr. Coello was shaking him. Seeing he was awake, he put his fingers to his lips, and pointed to the doorway, which was just an opening, without door, screen, or curtain.

Sonny got up and followed him outside.

Dr. Coello produced a bottle. Whisky.

"Get him drunk," he said.

So then Sonny knew for sure.

"When?" he asked.

"About an hour." Dr. Coello shrugged. "I looked while you were asleep. Get him drunk, that's all. Sometimes it helps. It can't do much harm." He touched Sonny's arm. "I'm sorry."

When Sonny went back in, Brother was sitting up on his side. He still looked wild-eyed but he wasn't delirious now. He seemed surrounded by some kind of still air that nothing in this world could move.

Sonny went over and poured a good stiff shot. There wasn't any point in pretending.

Brother drank it.

"Well, it's commendable whisky. Did I talk much?"

"When?"

"Last night." He waved with the glass to the cot. "Thanks for staying."

"It didn't make much sense."

"I don't suppose it did," said Brother, and held out an empty glass. He was careful not to look at him.

Sonny had forgotten how gentle Brother could be sometimes. He poured him another glass, and had some himself.

"Funny," said Brother. And looked round the room. "We do wind up in the strangest places."

Sonny couldn't say anything.

"You just got to talk, Sonny. You've just got to. I never was much good at talking. That's all."

So Sonny talked.

Between them they killed the bottle, almost.

Dr. Coello came in with a couple of peons and a stretcher.

Brother shook his head, and downed his whisky.

"I'd like to use them both, once more," he said, and smiled. "I don't care how much it hurts. I just want to use them once more, that's all."

Dr. Coello didn't say anything.

"Give me a hand, Sonny."

Sonny gave him a hand. It was the second time he'd ever touched Brother in his whole life. He didn't feel anything but fever.

They got down the corridor somehow.

"So this is it," said Brother, when they got to the room, just like the other room, where they'd spent the night. And got up on the table as though he didn't particularly care.

Sonny headed for the door.

"Stay," said Brother, and his voice wasn't steady at all. But you can't down most of a quart of whisky without some effects.

Sonny stayed, leaning well out of the way, against a wall.

A nurse came forward and there was a stench in the room. She had a wad of cotton in her hand, and the stench of chloroform filled the room, like those flowers in the courtyard, too heavy.

Well, you may want to vomit in a condition like that, but you don't. Brother struggled a bit, and then he went under.

The whole thing took about twenty minutes. But the sound of the saw wasn't exactly pretty. At home they'd butchered their own hogs. But they hadn't had a saw like this.

Dr. Coello folded the flap of skin back up, and sewed it, after cautery.

A funny smell, cautery. Like old leather burning.

Well, what else could he do? He picked up the leg by the calf (the amputation had been below the knee) and put it in a basket, and the nun took it away. But not before Sonny had had a good look at it. A real good look he never would forget.

And there was Brother, peaceful, but not complete any more. Just not complete.

What Sonny remembered about that leg was the toenails. Just the toenails.

They took Brother back to his room, and then Sonny walked through the town, that was all. Brother had liked to hunt, and ride, and be himself, and he was fixin' to marry Molly.

What Sonny could remember was the smell of the cautery. And the toenails.

On his way back, he stumbled into the big church, not that a church was what he was used to, he was used to a minister, if anything, but he went in anyway. It was big and damp. There wasn't anybody there but a bunch of black rebozoed women. Old women with wrinkles.

But candles were burning at a side altar, he didn't know to whom. He didn't care to whom. And he knelt down, and had one of those empty moments, he always had had from time to time in his life.

And then he went back, feeling as though both his own legs had been sliced through, maybe.

Garcias had found out what he wanted to know.

"They were hurt real bad."

"Both of them?"

"One of them had his leg cut off."

Navarro thought that over for a while. And then he just laughed and laughed. It really did appeal to his sense of humor. And it made him feel a lot better too.

The young one didn't count.

He'd gotten his revenge. Sideways. So he forgot, or almost forgot, all about it.

It had been the old one you had to worry about. He'd known that, as soon as he'd laid eyes on both of them.

Besides, he was safe in Chihuahua, wasn't he?

CHAPTER TWENTY-FIVE

ROTHER LAY propped up in his bed. He'd been there for a week now. Whatever else he did, he never looked under the covers.

One of the nuns had put a potted plant in the room. It was just a purple geranium. Mexicans love geraniums. But it had a funny smell.

Sonny had moved into a hotel. To judge by the night noises and the clientele, it was more than a hotel. He didn't have much truck with it. He wasn't in the mood. Most of the time he spent with Brother, not saying much, and then went back to bed.

He wasn't much taken with chippies. He wanted something else. But there was a girl there everybody called Maria. She didn't live in, and she wasn't a regular. He could tell that.

He couldn't stand just lying there every night, after seeing Brother. She didn't look too happy either. So he asked her in.

She was there the next night, too.

She was maybe about twenty-eight, and buxom and short. But she was clean, and at least he wasn't alone. She began to stay a while longer. She even seemed halfway to like him, in a cool, distant kind of a way. Why did she do it? Her man was dead. She had to live somehow.

"He used to send me money," she said. As though sending somebody money was the most affectionate thing in this world. Well, maybe it had been. He didn't know. He didn't much care.

It didn't satisfy him.

He kept thinking of Molly. And of Brother, just lying there, and not saying much.

He never did get the whole story. And there wasn't anything in it. It was just a sensation, that was all. Thursday it wasn't even that, so he didn't want her any more. Sonny felt pretty disgusted.

But he was so worn out he went to sleep anyway. Got up, had breakfast, and went over to Brother.

They both ignored that empty place under the bedclothes. But they couldn't really ignore it. Brother was in a bad way. And this time he went in, he'd just pulled up the sheets, and had a silly look on his face.

"It doesn't feel as though it's gone. It's the damndest thing," he said.

He tried to be cheerful, and then his voice would always trail off.

Brother wanted Sonny to go back home.

"The folks'll think we're dead. You go back, and then come down and get me in three weeks or a while."

Sonny shook his head.

"Maybe I'd like to be alone," said Brother.

"That isn't exactly what I've got in mind. I'm going to get him."

"You're crazy."

"I said I'm going to get him."

"They'll hang you," said Brother.

"What difference does that make?"

"If I can get over it, you can."

"I don't care. I'll take the chance."

"For Chrissake."

"I want to see him dead."

"Sis is dead, too. Who cares any more?"

"I care."

"Then let me handle it. What does it matter? I'm no good for anything any more. If they hang me, well, maybe it'd be better that way. But Annie might like to see you again."

"Nobody else would."

Brother looked as though he agreed. He'd been pretty depressed, and Sonny didn't blame him. And it was Sonny's fault, wasn't it?

"They tell me I can get around in a month. On crutches maybe. Or maybe I can get some old man to make me a wooden leg. Let me get 'im. One of us should get back in one piece."

"I'm taking you back."

"Maybe I don't want to go back."

"I'm taking you back."

Brother was very still. "I said maybe I don't want to. Don't you understand?"

"I didn't want to do it," said Sonny.

"You didn't do a damn thing, boy."

"I did."

"Let me get him and let them hang me," said Brother. "I'm no good for anything. Don't you think I know that?"

"You'll do."

Neither one of them mentioned what was really bothering Brother, which was Molly.

Sonny swallowed hard.

"I want to kill him myself," shouted Brother. "Don't you understand that?"

Yes, Sonny understood that. But he couldn't stand it. He just couldn't sit around. He had to do something.

He didn't know anybody but Maria, so when she was back at the hotel again that night, he started there. He met her on the stairs going up. He'd taken over Brother's Colt and had two holsters now, but that wasn't anything extraordinary. A lot of folks went round that way in Chihuahua. It wasn't exactly a settled town.

Besides, she was a girl who seemed to like people who went round like that, despite herself.

It was funny. In a crazy kind of way, he trusted her. He didn't exactly know why. He didn't trust her far. But he trusted her.

Tonight he lay on his back, on the bed, staring at the ceiling, wondering if he'd always be alone in hotel bedrooms like this. For after what he'd done to Brother and all, he knew he just plain never again could go home.

He couldn't ever go back and see the Prentices, or Molly.

He just had to ride and ride and never stop.

Maria was hard, of course. There wasn't anything in her. But she was a lot better than being alone, and he felt about fifty or sixty years old, and he couldn't ever do a thing to feel younger, now.

He kept remembering that leg.

"What are you thinking about?" she asked.

He turned over, and just cried like a baby, the way people do sometimes in a bed. But he didn't explain. Maybe he didn't exactly understand himself.

"Why did you come here?" she asked after a while.

Yeah, why? "You ever hear of a guy called Navarro?" he said, after a while. And felt her grow stiff.

"No," she said.

He turned over and slapped her. "You're lying," he said.

He slapped her real hard, over and over again.

After that, she just lay there.

"Why do you want to know?" she said at last. Her voice sounded hollow.

"I aim to kill him."

"It was he who shot your brother?"

"That's about it."

She didn't say anything for a long, long time. She just stared at the ceiling. He could practically hear the cogs in her head turning over.

Then she sighed.

"A lot of people would like to kill him," she said. "He is sometimes at a place called El Chico. Do you know it?"

He didn't know it.

"It is on the main street," she said. She didn't say anything else. Not until just before she was leaving.

"I won't see you any more," she said. "I don't know who you are. But I would like you to kill him."

Then she went out and left him alone.

CHAPTER TWENTY-SIX

H E DIDN'T KNOW what the story was there. But apparently he'd hit something.

He went quietly about the business and didn't tell Brother a thing. Not just yet, anyhow. What he was going to do required a little thought.

So he thought about it. And after a while, he had a plan. After a considerable while, because Sonny didn't exactly have quick thoughts. He just acted quick.

Navarro knew what he looked like.

So that meant he had to look like somebody else.

When he really put his mind to it, and had an object in view, Sonny could be downright methodical.

Hair grows at the rate of a quarter of an inch a month. But he grew sideburns, and in two weeks they were okay. A mustache was harder. That took a month. At the end of that time, nobody would have known him, not his own mother. Though he found it hard to think of Annie as his mother. Annie was Annie, that was all.

Brother watched this little growth without much comment. He was feeling better, and therefore restless, but he still didn't want to get out of that bed. To get out of that bed meant he'd have to accept that he just had one leg.

The skin flap was beginning to heal, and it itched.

Brother was real quiet these days. He just had that funny, lopsided, absent-minded smile. Which about cut Sonny's heart out, so something had to be done.

When the sideburns and the mustache were well grown, and with that suntan, despite his height, he might have been a local. He went out shopping.

He knew his way round Chihuahua by now. Like any city, it wasn't so big, once you got used to it. There was a street for this and a street for that. And the tailors all lived up the end of alleys, downstairs. He and Brother were running low on cash, because though the doctor hadn't taken a fee, he'd suggested a contribution to the nuns, which they'd tried to make generous, but there was enough cash left, just the same. Enough and no more, but they could live on the country, going back.

So Sonny invested in various goods at various grinning cross-legged tailors, dragged the stuff back to his hotel, and had himself a dress rehearsal in front of the wardrobe mirror.

The result wasn't bad: black bell-bottomed trousers, split at the ankles, one of those high riding, tight fitting, braid-trimmed Mexican jackets that cut you under the arms, and a big, broad-brimmed Mexican sombrero. What with the sideburns and the mustache, except that his eyes were blue, his own mother wouldn't have known him.

Sonny had noticeable eyes, the sort of eyes you slowly become aware of, somewhere in the room, staring you down. They were very pale, very blue, and it wasn't as though they were staring at you, but as though someone were staring at you through them, from a long, long way. Then he'd blink and shift his gaze. Sonny blinked a lot, particularly outdoors, where the hard light hurt his eyelids and made his eyes feel grainy. It was a nervous habit he had.

But even if you forgot him, you remembered the eyes.

There wasn't much he could do about that, not even being aware of it.

He grinned at himself and slouched out into the hall, to try the disguise out in the street. There he ran into Maria. He hadn't seen her for days, and she didn't recognize him.

He pulled her arm, and said, "Hey." She went off into a torrent of Spanish before she recognized him. And then she began to laugh.

There wasn't any relaxation in the laugh at all.

"Well, what's so funny?" he wanted to know.

"Nothing," she said. "Nothing. I didn't even recognize you."

"That was sort of the idea," he told her, and waltzed himself down the stairs. He was feeling pretty good.

It was early yet, only about eight-thirty, and wherever Navarro was hanging out, Sonny didn't think he'd find him at El Chico just yet. He went in there anyway, and had a drink, but the place was half empty. There was only one other man at his end of the bar, and they didn't speak.

It was Garcias, but Sonny didn't even know who Garcias was.

He drank up, went outside, looked up and down the street, which was crowded with that usual sauntering crowd any Mexican town always has on a warm evening, and headed for the hospital, still feeling frisky.

The corridor was dim. He slipped into Brother's room. Brother was lying on his back, not doing anything in particular. But he'd asked for his gun back a week ago, and slept with it under his pillow.

He snatched it out now. The holster and belt fell to the floor. Maimed or not, there wasn't anything wrong with Brother's draw.

"Hey, it's me," said Sonny.

Brother put the gun down. "Of all the damn-fool tricks," he said. "Why the getup?"

"Well, you didn't recognize me, did you?"

"You never know who's going to come in here," said Brother. "They must know we're here."

"They don't know nothing."

"You going after him like that?"

"I found out where he hangs out. I thought I'd go looking."

"You know how I feel about that."

"I've heard tell," said Sonny. "But I want all of them. And I want him."

"Tonight?"

"If I can find him."

Brother handed his Colt over. "Good luck," he said. And lay down on his back again.

Sonny went out through the courtyard, and then headed downhill, towards the main street.

CHAPTER TWENTY-SEVEN

Rounding a good gang up always takes a while. You have to know who's going to be good and who's going to be no damn good at all, and it's the ones who are no damn good at all who are the first to volunteer. The others you have to go look for yourself.

Navarro figured he needed about ten men. So far, not counting Garcias, he'd rounded up four. And he was getting tired of the waiting round. He wanted to get out of here, and on the road again, and besides, he was still worried about those gringos. He hadn't seen them round, but you never knew. If you stay in one place too long, somebody's bound to take a shot at you.

Right now he was at Maria's, only she didn't know it yet. She hadn't come back from wherever she was, and he sat there drinking the place out. What he was there for was to make her an offer. Maria had been Pedro's girl. You have to keep your hands off something in this world, to keep things running smoothly, so Navarro had kept his hands off her. But he'd always wanted her. He'd heard she'd gone back to hustling, now Pedro was dead, and anything was better than that. So he didn't think she'd put up much of a fight, now he wanted her.

He made himself right at home. He always did. There was a pot of chili on the stove, so he ate it. There was some tequila, so he drank it. By midevening he was pretty liquored up.

She didn't come back until late. There weren't any windows on the street side of her house, if you could call two rooms a house, so she wasn't prepared for his being there.

By that time he'd moved into the bedroom and eased his belt. He was a fat man, and he'd eaten too much chili. So he lay on the bed, drinking happily.

He heard her come in, and smiled. She was in for a surprise. She came right to the bedroom. She was flushed, as though she'd been in a hurry, but that only made her prettier.

"Oh, you," she said.

"Is that all you've got to say?"

"Isn't that enough? Get out of here."

"Maria," he said. "I just wanted to be friendly." He got off the bed and came towards her. She backed away.

"Don't you like me?"

"I want you out of here."

"I stay," he said. And tried to grab hold of her. He always knew where he stood with women. He knew he was stronger than they were. But she surprised him. She managed to wrench away.

He blinked, surprised.

"Do you think I'd have anything to do with you? Why don't you get back to Concepción?"

"You're prettier."

"If you come near me I'll kill you," she shouted.

Navarro shrugged. He liked a little fight. "Pedro's dead," he said. "What difference does it make? He never gave you much. I could give you plenty."

"You killed him."

"What gives you that idea?"

"Garcias told me."

"Garcias talks too damn much."

"He was going to marry me."

"Someday." Navarro sounded contemptuous. Why did they always want to get married, anyhow?

"When he got back."

"He's dead now. So what?"

"I loved him."

"Well, now you can love me. I'm not so bad."

She ran into the kitchen and picked up the knife she used to cut meat. He wasn't scared. He knew he'd get her round. He always got what he wanted. But Garcias shouldn't have spilled the beans that way. He wiped his mouth and ambled towards her, keeping a sharp eye on that knife. Maybe if he shot it out of her hand, she might feel differently.

But he was drunk. His aim wasn't so good. It took him three shots to do it.

Then he took his time about it. Nobody was going to worry about a shooting in that neighborhood. Keeping between her and the door to the street, he moved up in his own good time. He felt slow but excited. He liked them with some fight in them.

She lost her head and ran into the bedroom.

Then he knew he had her.

Sonny headed for El Chico. It was the biggest cantina in town, a double room, Mexican style, with two striped poles to hold the middle of the roof up, a bar along one wall, one or two tables, the cloths on them flyblown, and a passageway to a court-yard out in back. The place was packed solid, but he didn't see Navarro there.

He waited round for an hour or so. He didn't dare ask direct where the bastard was. He had to hedge around. And he also had to explain himself. He said he was a rancher's son from New Mexico. That explained the accent okay.

He managed to give the impression he was loaded with cash. There's nothing like baiting your own trap. He let on as how he was looking for a little excitement. But mostly he didn't talk too much. He just watched.

Still no Navarro.

It made him jumpy, but he didn't think he'd been recognized. He did every dive on the main street, and a good many up back alleys, until, though he tried not to drink much, he was beginning to feel a mite drunk. But he didn't find Navarro anywhere.

At one-thirty he decided to call it a night and try again tomorrow. He made it up the stairs to his room, headed for the bed, and passed out.

Maria lay on the bed and didn't say anything.

"You just learn to behave and you'll do fine," said Navarro. He liked them when they fought.

He started to drink again, when there was a knock on the outside door. Maybe because he was tired, he felt jumpy. He let her answer it.

It was just Garcias.

He slipped into the room, past Maria.

"Hell I've been looking all over for you. Lopez waited for you at El Chico. He's pretty mad."

"Who's Lopez?"

"He used to be with Guerrero. He heard you were looking for somebody."

"Tell him I'll be there tomorrow."

"You know those Americans you asked me about?"

"Yeah." Navarro felt a funny feeling in his stomach. It was just a feeling.

"Well, the old one's in the hospital all right. But the other one's disappeared."

"What do you mean he's disappeared?"

"He ain't at the hospital any more, that's all."

Navarro thought that over. "You'd better ask round," he said.

"You going to stay here?"

"No."

Garcias looked at both of them, and then grinned to himself. Maria could have slapped him. She knew what he was thinking. He was thinking when one dies, you get another one.

But she wasn't quite like that.

When they had gone, she sat there, rubbing her arms, and thinking things over.

Then she smiled, too. Tomorrow she'd go to the hotel.

Everybody knew she was working out of there. Nobody would see anything odd in that.

CHAPTER TWENTY-EIGHT

SONNY SPENT most of the morning and afternoon staying in his room. So he was there when the rap came on the door. He wasn't expecting anybody. You can't be too careful. He didn't answer it.

"It's me. Maria."

He let her in.

She looked determined. "Navarro," she said. "He'll be at the cantina tonight."

It could be a trap, but somehow he didn't think so. And he didn't much care whether it was or not. Just so he could get Navarro, that was all that mattered.

After Maria'd gone, he went over to Brother.

"Still alive, I see," said Brother.

"I missed him. He's going to be there tonight."

"So this is it?"

"This is it."

Brother sighed. "It's been a long ride," he said. "A long ride. You sure you want to do it this way?"

"There isn't any other way."

"I told you how I felt about that."

"No. I'll see to it."

There wasn't anything else to say. He got up to go.

"Take care of yourself," said Brother.

It was like talking to a stranger.

How does a man with one leg feel, anyhow?

Sonny hit the bar about ten. There wasn't any point in getting there early. But he wanted it over with. He couldn't hang round doing nothing for the rest of his life.

He forced himself to walk to El Chico as though he didn't have a worry in the world. He wanted to take this slow and easy.

He needn't have worried. The place was jammed.

Too jammed to shoot. Too jammed to see anything. He pushed his way in, to the door end of the bar, and ordered whisky. He should have called for tequila, but if he was going to shoot it out, he wanted whisky.

The bartender poured in person. In Chihuahua, whisky was an important drink. Besides, he was a stranger, and everybody's always curious about a stranger, bartenders most of all.

It was a different bartender than last night.

Sonny took it all in and suddenly he felt tired. More tired than he'd ever felt in his life before. He wondered what the hell he was doing here, anyhow. Back home life was a lot simpler.

He wondered what Annie was doing right now.

And Molly.

Well, it didn't do any good to think. He downed the whisky, which was vile, worse than homebrew, but it kicked you so hard, you didn't worry none, which was some help.

There was a funny feeling in the place tonight. He couldn't quite pin it down. Maybe he'd brought it with him. He kept to himself and went on drinking.

Then, looking up, he saw two men come in through the courtyard. He didn't know the other one but the fat one was Navarro all right.

It wasn't a place to shoot it out in. He just wanted Navarro. He didn't want to cause any unnecessary pain. He'd have to wait until they left and then follow.

"Where's Lopez?" asked Navarro.

"He'll be along."

"Nobody keeps Navarro waiting."

"I said he'll be along," said Garcias.

Navarro grunted and headed for the bar. He never ordered for himself. That's why he needed someone like Garcias. You can't be a big man unless you've got a little man to run your errands for you.

It was one of Navarro's beer nights. Garcias ordered beer.

Navarro felt pretty good. Another week, he figured, and he could pull out of here. Also he felt pretty good about last night. Show a woman where she stands, and you've got her where you want her.

It was one big joke on Pedro anyway.

Time passed. But Lopez still didn't show up, and Navarro got fidgety. His eyes started to rove over the bar.

And so he spotted Sonny, down at the end, staring right back at him. The light was dim. Navarro couldn't exactly see him. But there was something that made him stand out.

"Who's he?"

Garcias shrugged. "Some crazy rancher's son from New Mexico. At least that's what he says."

"He looks like a gringo."

Garcias just shrugged again.

"I don't like strangers. When did he show up?"

"Last night."

"I don't like it."

"He's just drinking quietly, that's all."

"I said I don't like it. Go find out who he is."

"I told you, that's who he is."

Navarro didn't feel right about it. "You find out where the other guy went, the one with the guy at the hospital?"

Garcias hadn't.

Navarro felt sure of his own ground here. But he was curious. He had to know. And every damn time he looked up, he seemed to see that man, down at the far end of the bar. Finally it got too much for him.

Sonny had thought maybe it might. He just went on staring, from time to time. He could tell Navarro was getting restless. He couldn't shoot in here. If he did, the crowd would tear him to pieces. He had to figure some way of getting him outside.

He looked down at his glass.

When he looked up again, Navarro was staring at him, with an odd look on his face. Their eyes locked, and as Sonny looked away, Navarro began to edge his way down the crowded room.

So all he had to do was wait. This was it.

"I'm going to find out who that guy is," said Navarro.

"Why bother? Lopez will be here in a minute..."

"To hell with Lopez. Come on."

For some reason, Garcias didn't want to come on. He looked round the room, gulped, and did as he was told.

Navarro took his time about it. This was his hangout. He didn't have any anxieties exactly. But he didn't like strangers.

Sonny watched them come. And then there the stinking greaseball was, right in front of him, half drunk, with a wet-pants look on his face, except that it was a dangerous face. He might be a proved coward, but you couldn't underestimate him, just the same. Never underestimate a coward.

"Do I know you, yes?" asked Navarro. It wasn't exactly a polite question.

Sonny didn't reckon so, in his very best Spanish.

"Where you from?"

"New Mexico."

Navarro grunted. "I've seen you some place before."

"That you have. Several times." Sonny didn't look at him directly, but he knew he had him bothered. He stood there, waiting.

"But where? I do not remember where."

Sonny was all of a sudden very conscious of those Colts round his waist. The thing to do was get him outside.

"Just places," he said. "You'll be seeing me again, too, I guess." Then, very deliberately, he turned and walked out, wondering whether he'd get shot in the back or not. But somehow he didn't think so.

Men like Navarro like to do their shooting up a back alley.

He went through the batwing doors, hoping they'd follow. But he couldn't turn round to see. He went right on walking, past somebody standing just outside, he didn't even have time to notice who, and out into the street.

It was pretty late, the crowd had thinned out considerable. So it was here or nowhere.

"Gringo, come back. When Navarro asks a question, his question gets answered," he heard behind him.

So this was it. The end of the whole damn mess. Sonny started to turn round, very slowly, until he was facing him. Pretend to be peaceable.

It would be his luck, to have himself right in the light from the cantina, while they were in shadow. But they were both there, Garcias and Navarro.

He drew fast.

Navarro must have recognized him, at last, because he got a funny look on his face and didn't draw quite fast enough.

That was his hard luck. Sonny had gotten to be a mighty fast draw recently.

Garcias got a shot out, before he crumpled. Navarro didn't. The impact of the lead made them wobble on their feet, and then they went down.

Everybody scattered.

Sonny went up to them, and emptied the rest of his right gun into Navarro. He owed Brother that much. But it didn't make him feel much better. It was just over, that was all.

Then he kicked Garcias over, and shot him with the left gun, once, very neatly in the forehead.

So that was the end of it. The end of Sis. The end of the whole damn hunt. The end for Brother. Except nobody wasn't ever going to give Brother back that leg of his.

He stood there for a second, looking down. Because it wasn't the end of it. It didn't help at all.

Everything's so motionless, after a shooting. Everything is so quiet. Until the tension breaks.

Maria came down the steps from the cantina, took a good look at Navarro, spat, and then grabbed Sonny.

"This way," she said. "This way." And rushed him over to an alley. They both ran down it, as fast as they could go.

Sonny didn't stop to ask questions. Besides, he hadn't the breath.

The alley made an elbow bend. They reached it, and saw an open street in front of them. Then the opening was blocked with Rurales.

There wasn't any point in turning back. Sonny gave himself up. After all, what did it matter now?

CHAPTER TWENTY-NINE

M ARIA THEY LET GO. They may not have believed her story, there was always more in these things than you ever heard about, but they let her go. But not before Sonny had told her to get Dr. Coello. He didn't know anybody else to send for.

Because Sonny they kept.

One thing about Mexicans, they don't go in for spur of the moment street lynchings. But there sure as hell isn't much you can say for a Mexican jail.

And this was his second one. If anything, it was even smellier than the first. He put in a bad night in a single cell. The other Mexicans on either side of him wouldn't talk much. He'd shot Navarro. That made him a big shot. But he was a gringo. So that meant they didn't trust him.

He wasn't sorry he'd done it. Navarro had had it coming. But it hadn't settled anything. All that mattered now was to get Brother out of here and back to Molly.

What he'd do after that, he didn't know.

In the morning they routed him out and fed him breakfast, which meant polenta and coffee. The polenta tasted like paste. What the coffee tasted like was nobody's business. They wouldn't even let him send out for a barber. He was a dangerous American. He had to be kept where he was.

About ten o'clock they took him out, down the corridor, with a guard on either side, very official. Otherwise it was about like Juarez.

He must look silly in this local getup by now. Certainly he felt silly. If they were going to hang him, he wanted to be hanged in his own clothes.

What he got instead was another official, older than the one in Juarez, shrewder, probably even more corrupt. But the tone was different. Sonny could tell that right away. Juarez was on the border. There every case was a dangerous case, touch and go.

But Chihuahua was a law-abiding town, and apparently he'd broken the law.

"You call it breaking the law, shooting down a bandit like that?" asked Sonny.

"Ah, you speak Spanish," said the officer. He seemed relieved.

"You bet I speak Spanish. You call that murder?"

The officer shrugged. "We shall not miss him. But we do not like shootings in the street, either."

Sonny just made a noise.

"You and your friend," said the officer patiently.

"What friend?"

"The man in the hospital."

"He's my brother. He doesn't have anything to do with it."

"With this, perhaps not. But I do not think you came here peaceably." He did not look comfortable. Mexican-American relations were difficult enough. He did not want an incident. "If you had any valid reason ..."

"What's that?"

"Why did you do it?"

Sonny told him. He told him all of it, from Sis, right down through that awful, endless ride, right down to Brother's accident and amputation. He didn't leave out a thing. It took him quite a while.

"You do not have a permit to be in Mexico," said the man, who was a colonel. In Mexico the police and the military seemed to get mixed up. Or maybe they were about the same thing.

Talking Spanish that long had made Sonny tired. He didn't even know whether he was understood.

"Who needs a permit? Did he need a permit to come riding up into our land and rape my sister?"

"If that is true, the killing can be written off as justified," said the colonel. "But that remains to be seen."

"I just told you, didn't I?"

"Navarro would have told me something else."

"Right now he isn't exactly in a position to tell anybody anything."

"Exactly," said the colonel.

Sonny might have known. There wasn't any use in talking. He didn't have a chance. So he'd have to make his own chance. Just how he was going to do that, he didn't know.

He let them take him back to his cell. And there he stayed, all morning, with his hands up to the bars, looking out the window, at the dusty plaza in front of whatever this building was. Over the roofs he could make out the dome and the towers of the church, and wondered how Brother was getting along.

Ten to one they'd arrest him too.

An American jail, it's a small, poky building, and besides, everybody speaks your own language. Here the walls were thick and they'd been here a long time.

His only hope now was Dr. Coello.

But Dr. Coello didn't come and didn't come, and the day went slowly. After noon the shadows in the plaza outside got deeper and longer.

Sonny felt just about fit to be tied.

One thing, if he got out of here, nobody was ever going to get him locked up again. That he'd make sure of. He paced up and down his cell angrily. They'd put him in a different section than he'd been in the night before. There at least you could look left and right, through the bars, into the other cells. This cell had solid walls and an iron door with a sliding panel in it. He was fed through that. That was the only time he saw the jailer, let alone anybody else, and the silence got on his nerves. He hadn't anything to watch but the plaza outside, through that high-up window even he had to stand on his toes to look out of.

His plan, when Coello came, if he ever did come, was to get him to get somebody to ride north, to just west of El Paso, where some United States Dragoons were camped, and tell their captain the Henshaws were in trouble and needed help. It wasn't such a crazy plan. Ever since the Mexican War, there'd been a lot of traffic over the borderlands. Chihuahua was pretty far south, but it had been occupied by Americans during the war, which was only eight years ago, and it wasn't that far south.

He couldn't think of anything else to do. It was a simple matter of justice, that was all. If he couldn't get it, he'd take it, and the Dragoons would come, he was pretty sure of that. In the borderlands Americans could be trusted to take care of their own.

But Chihuahua *was* pretty far south. And Coello just plain didn't come.

It drove Sonny nearly bats.

Just before sunset, he heard the clatter of horses out in the square and some shouting that sounded mighty like American. He ran to the window and hoisted himself up and couldn't believe his eyes. A whole detachment of American cavalry was going by outside, in full dress, pennants flying. It came out of the shadows at one end of the square and was jogging into the shadows at the other. Sonny shouted and tried to wave. But they couldn't see him. They didn't seem to hear him. They were making too damn much racket to hear anybody. Not one of them looked up.

He thought maybe he was having delusions or something. When he looked again, the plaza was empty. He went to the iron cell door, and banged on it. But nobody came. He shouted. Nobody paid any attention.

He just had to sit there.

It drove him half crazy.

CHAPTER THIRTY

NEXT MORNING was about the same. He woke early and it was the longest morning he'd ever spent. The jailer fed him that polenta mush again, but just slammed the judas window on him when he asked to see the colonel, Coello, anybody. There wasn't a thing he could do but sit there and wait.

It was funny, though they'd taken away his Colts, they'd let him keep the holsters. The empty holsters made him feel worse amputated than Brother was. One thing, if he ever got them back, and got out of here, he'd never let them take him again, and he'd never move without a gun. Being shut up drove him half wild. Even when he was small, he'd done everything to avoid being shut in. He didn't like to be pinned down. He didn't like to be shoved around.

Probably they'd dragged Brother out of his bed, and had him locked up somewhere in this rattrap, too, for all he knew.

By midafternoon he was beating his fists against the door and cursing his head off. It didn't do any good. All he did was cut his hands. He sat down on the bed and looked at them.

And was still looking at them when the bolt on the door shot back, and the door opened. He'd about given up hope, but he looked to see if it was Coello. It wasn't. Just the jailer and a couple of Rurales, spic and span, and heavily armed, as though he were a criminal.

They walked behind him this time, maybe so if he made a break for it they could have the pleasure of shooting him in the back. He decided not to give them that pleasure. He walked stolidly ahead, looking for a chance, just one chance, to get out of there.

They didn't give it to him. He was marched along the same corridors, and back to the same room he'd been in before.

Only this time, when he went in, Coello was there, and a man he'd never seen before, a major in the United States cavalry, to judge by the look of him. Those yellow-striped blue pants were sure a welcome sight.

The Mexican colonel didn't look happy. "This is Major Hunt," he said. "Major Hunt has persuaded me to let you go. He confirms your story."

Sonny ignored him. Somehow he didn't think the truth of the story had much to do with it one way or the other. One thing he'd learned, this ride, was when it comes to a pinch, it helps to have a gun. People may mean well, but if you want to keep your skin, you've got to lean on them a little.

But it wasn't exactly the time to be outspoken. He turned to Coello instead.

"Where's my brother?" he asked.

"In the hospital."

"He okay?"

Coello nodded.

"I want you both out of here and headed north as soon as possible," said the colonel.

"Delighted to oblige," said Sonny. "Only I'd like my guns back this time."

The colonel frowned. But, Sonny had to admit, it was a considerable improvement over Juarez, he did get the guns back. When he got them slipped into their holsters, he felt a lot better. When they were loaded he'd feel even better yet. But this maybe wasn't exactly the place to see to that.

Coello and Hunt watched that little pantomime without saying anything. There were a few courtesies. Then they went out down the hall, turned left this time, and there he was, actually a free man, standing on the steps of that plaza that had seemed a million miles away, for the last two days.

It wasn't going to be any trouble to leave Chihuahua, not at all. He never wanted to see it again.

Major Hunt was a thick-set, spruce man of about forty. His name was Ben.

"You're a lucky boy, son," he said. "I don't mind telling you that the colonel in there took considerable persuading. Even so, you're in my custody until we reach the border."

"Glad of the company," said Sonny, and realized he could use a shave. And his own clothes back, and all.

Hunt didn't seem particularly to care for that line of talk.

"There'll be a ruckus, of course," he said. "You can't do what you boys did, and get away with it. But I guess it'll blow over. There isn't much they can do about it, now you're out." Then he chuckled. "I was talking to your brother. It's quite a story at that."

Sonny seemed to make him uneasy.

"Nice man, your brother," he said. "It's a damn shame about his leg."

Coello suggested they'd better keep off the streets. Hunt saw them as far as the hospital, made arrangements, and went off to his men.

Coello didn't seem to have much to say to Sonny either. You'd think he was a pariah or something. But Sonny didn't care. He was out now. He sidled into Brother's room.

"Well, I got 'im," he said.

"So I heard," said Brother dryly. But he looked glad to see him, just the same.

"Who's this guy Hunt?"

"He's what you might call your lucky break. He was on his way back from Mexico City, to pay the purchase money for the Mesilla Valley. Otherwise you might have stayed in that jail a long, long time. How'd they treat you?"

"It's over now," said Sonny, feeling tired, and having a feeling a lot more was over than just this, though he didn't have any idea what.

He just felt lost, that was all.

A nun came in, carrying something long and bright yellow with varnish. She said something with that awful sickroom cheerfulness some people seem to think makes you feel better.

Brother blushed and looked shy. "I've had a man whittle me some crutches," he said. "I got to practice." He wriggled himself round in the bed, and one leg, the whole one, came out from under the covers, and felt round for the floor.

"I'd like to be alone for a while. I haven't got the hang of it yet," said Brother.

Sonny went very quickly out of the room.

When he came back in an hour, Brother was back in bed.

"It won't be so bad," he said, and that didn't help either. Because though Brother was smiling, there was something awful lost and hurt in his eyes.

Next morning, at down, the cavalry came down the street, and Hunt and Sonny got Brother boosted onto a horse somehow. If you saw him from the left side, he looked just about the way he'd always looked, only maybe older. The right leg was amputated far enough down, so he could get a grip on the saddle okay. But the only place to put the crutches was in the rifle holster of the saddle, and there wasn't any missing those. Why did they have to be that bright yellow color? It looked raw.

It was a slow trip back, over about the same trail they'd come down by. Slow and uneventful, except that Hunt wanted to have them talk it all out, the way it had happened, every time they came to a place like the canyon, for instance, where Brother's troubles had begun.

After all, it was quite a story. Only Sonny wanted to forget it, and he guessed Brother did too.

They went through Juarez in a tight little clump, and parted at El Paso. Brother's leg still needed attention. They'd rest up there for a week or so.

Since Hunt was going north anyway, Brother wrote a note to Annie, to prepare her, and let her know they weren't dead, and asked Sonny to take it along to the camp.

"Is that all? Just Annie?" Sonny asked.

"Yeah. Just Annie."

So then Sonny knew for sure what he'd been pretty sure of all along, ever since Brother had been delirious. But there wasn't anything he could say about it.

Brother's manner didn't exactly encourage talk.

CHAPTER THIRTY-ONE

TWO WEEKS to rest up, and they got on their way. The trouble is, there was just one way, unless you made a long detour round the mountains, the trail that led back the way they'd come, through Agua Prieta, Naco, the Canelo Hills, and down through Lochiel.

Brother didn't say anything. Brother never would say anything. But it would be their luck that when they hit Lochiel, it was a fine morning, the air was clear, there were birds singing, and the place looked more than ever lush, and green, and like a paradise.

So it was up to Sonny to do something. He turned his horse north, towards the valley, the Prentice place, and Molly. But Brother wouldn't let him get away with that.

"Where the hell do you think you're headed?"

"Taking you where you belong."

Brother shook his head. "We go on," he said. "We just go on."

Sonny tried to take the reins of Brother's horse.

Brother stared him down. "I said we go on. You let go of those reins, or I'll shoot you. I mean it."

"For Pete's sake, don't you think..."

"I mean it, Sonny. What I think's my own business. We go on."

So they went on.

Though for the rest of the day Brother was careful to ride ahead, where he couldn't be seen, until they were well away from there.

It took Annie a while, after she got the letter. She just sat alone with it, getting used to it, before she told Pa. But she'd been nearly frantic. And at least they'd both be back. At least they weren't dead. And Sonny was all right. That was something.

She couldn't help it if she thought of Sonny first. But poor Adrian. And she knew Adrian, even if they didn't get along too well. There went everything, as far as he was concerned, she knew that. She thought of writing to Molly. But no, he wouldn't like that. He'd handle it his own way.

They'd be back in a week, that was what counted. That was the thing to think about. A week would be next Friday or Saturday. And then sat waiting. She went to tell Pa.

Friday afternoon, late, she saw a horse and rider in the distance, coming from the direction of the Cunningham place. Just one horse, one rider. That scared her. She couldn't tell what that meant.

But after watching for half an hour, she saw it was a woman, one of the Cunningham girls probably. The Cunninghams knew the boys were coming back. It was nice of them to come over to help.

The rider came closer and closer, drew up, and slid down to the ground. It was nobody Annie had ever seen before, but it was somebody she liked the look of, right away, and she had a feeling before she knew, so when Molly introduced herself, Annie wasn't exactly surprised.

Major Hunt had been at the Prentice place. There was nothing out of the way in that. Down in that part of the country, the Prentice place was the one place to go. He had a few stories to tell, and that one of them was a story the Prentices weren't exactly glad to hear wasn't anything any of them was going to tell him. And how like Adrian not to let on that he even knew the Prentices. So now they knew why they hadn't heard.

Molly thought that over for a week. Then she saddled a horse and announced where she was going.

"You sure you know what you're doing?"

"Yes."

"Well, I can't say I think you're wrong. When you're both up to it, bring him back here. And good luck," said her father, and stood on the veranda, watching, until she was well out of sight.

Molly didn't see any point in bothering Annie with all that. There wasn't any call to.

Together they kept watch, all next day, without anyone turning up, and then Sunday morning and Sunday afternoon.

At about dusk, they saw two riders come over the ridge, and down towards the valley, very slowly.

"I'll stay in the kitchen," said Molly, smoothing down her dress. "You go outside."

Annie understood that. She went outside, shielding her eyes with her hand. The riders moved so slowly down the hillside, she thought she'd have to stand there forever. Sonny had a peculiar erect way of holding himself in the saddle. She could recognize him, all right, even a quarter of a mile away.

She wanted to wave, but she couldn't. She felt too much like crying. And she knew she mustn't flinch when she saw what had happened to Adrian, she mustn't show anything. So she squared her shoulders and went on watching.

Then, as she watched, that tall figure turned back.

"This is as far as I go," said Sonny.

Brother looked surprised.

"I'm not coming down." Sonny stared towards the farmstead. "I can't, that's all."

"Don't be a bloody fool. You think you're to blame for anything?"

Sonny got that funny, shy, stubborn look in his eyes he always got when you tried to pin him down about anything. Maybe he wasn't so unlike Brother after all.

He sat there on his horse, taking a good, long, slow look at that small figure down there, waiting outside the house, at the pine tree, the graveyard, at everything he'd ever lived with. And then he turned his horse's head and rode back up the ridge, until he disappeared over it.

An outlaw, they say. But conscience can be a peculiar thing.

Brother looked after him, and then went on down the hill.